MOON STRUCK

THE THIRD LUNAR LOVESCAPE NOVEL

ESSIE POWERS

WORKOUT SCHEDULE

L *an Niu tightened her grip* on the pair of twenty-five kilo dumbbells. She felt all the muscles in her forearms tighten.

Her biceps and triceps were prone; ready to *pump some iron*. She took a deep breath in before blowing it right back out.

She waited.

From above her hairline, from within the tightly bound bun into which she had swept her sleek black hair, a single bead of sweat rolled down from her temple. It trickled down her cheek. Settled on the razor-sharp line of her chin. It clung on for several seconds.

Then it dropped.

The second she heard the minute *splash* on the mat below, she tensed every muscle in her body, turning her attention to the mass which needed to be lifted.

The current task which needed to be completed.

She managed ten repetitions before allowing the dumbbells to drop back onto the rubber grips of the spotter stand. A quiver ran across the surface of her body.

She breathed in a shuddering breath, then exhaled.

She rocked herself up into a sitting position.

Then she glanced about her surroundings, to the gym, located on one of the lower floors of the employee residences known as the Basements.

She was alone here; she was *always* alone at this time.

That was the reason she picked this time at all.

Everyone else would be going about their late-morning duties.

Lan had made a point of assigning her gym time to this particular slot.

She had realised, a long time ago, that she didn't get along well with other people, and so she had taken the executive decision to keep herself apart from the herd. That was probably one of the reasons why she'd ended up on the Moon; why she'd ended up signing a contract with Celestial Stays. It was a way for her to get away from Earth; a way for her to get away from reality. A way for her to get away from her *parents*.

She winced.

It annoyed and surprised her in equal measure to realise that *they* still exercised a hold on her; that even up on the lunar surface they managed to affect her.

Back home—if she could still call it that—back in *Shanghai*, her parents had brought her up with one aim, and one aim *only*. That when she hit the lower age limit for applications she would join the Republic of China Air Force—the ROCAF—and so follow in her mother and father's footsteps.

Her father had made Colonel, while her mother had one-upped him when she was promoted to Brigadier General. So the expectations placed on Lan were understandably high.

However, when, at seventeen—and with a whole childhood in the Cadets behind her; and the whole weight of parental expectation resting on her shoulders—she had gone through the standard medical tests, as required for those wishing to join the ROCAF, she had been instantly rejected on medical grounds.

She had what the examining medical officer had described as a 'minor heart defect'.

The worst part hadn't been the actual moment when the medical officer had declared her Unfit for Service; the worst part had been the weeks—and *months*—which'd followed the failed medical test. How her parents had seemingly petitioned every last person they possibly could.

Lan had even heard rumours that her mother and father had attempted to gain an audience with the President herself . . . but, assuming from the outcome, Lan's non-acceptance into the ROCAF, they had been denied.

It was all so clear in Lan's mind, how she had entered a sort of purgatory. Since at that time, for the first time in her life, she had no schooling to attend to, she had made a point of getting out of the house for as much of the day as she could manage. She had found solace in the many libraries located around Shanghai, and she spent a good long while in the parks. Her favourite by far, and the one which she found herself constantly returning to, was Fuxing Park. Its French-style fountains, pavilions and placid lake had offered a moment's peace from the hustle and bustle of the city. However, following further medical tests—the many strenuous examinations her parents put Lan through in a hopeless effort to get her accepted into the ROCAF—Lan had been cleared to continue exercising. And that was when she had discovered the gym.

It seemed the largest turning point in her life. Lan at age seventeen had always been slightly underweight—*somewhat weedy*. And it was then, following the failed medical examination, that she had found a determination from somewhere within her to make a change; to *transform* into someone else entirely. To begin with it was clearly because she'd wanted to prove her parents wrong. She had wanted to *show* them that she didn't need to walk the same path they had walked. That she could cut her own way through the foliage and find her own trail.

But, soon enough, the gym had become something else to her; it had taken on an entirely different meaning. Because it was among the elaborate—*heavy*—equipment that Lan could force her mind somewhere else; that she could truly *escape* from her day-to-day responsibilities. That she could find out who she was for herself.

Although her parents' disappointment at her failing to join the ROCAF would never entirely be overcome, they were somewhat placated by Lan's acceptance to Tongji University to study aeronautical engineering. Even from the start of the course, Lan was deeply aware that she had signed up for all the wrong reasons; that she was doing it only as a desperate, final attempt to make her parents proud. She had lasted hardly longer than the first semester before dropping out.

It was easy to pin down that particular moment as being the one which'd led to an all-time low in her relationship with her parents.

Actually, to tell the truth, she hadn't seen them since the day she had packed all the bare essentials into a tight, gym bag; wished them well; and then, without another word, stepped out of the door, and out of their lives. She hadn't even had contact. Not so much as a message.

Lan knew that her mother—being the most stubborn of her

parents—would have been preventing her father from writing to her. She could imagine her father itching to write her a letter; to ask how she was doing; to ask how she was *getting on* outside of the only world they knew in the Air Force.

For them, a career outside the Air Force was just as alien of a concept as accepting a contract to work on the Moon was for Lan.

She wondered if her parents would be proud of her now; thirty-two years old, and with no sign of her settling down in any one place; no sign of her *maturing* into herself.

In any case, what would it matter to her parents?

For them she had already committed the ultimate failure.

And she would never be redeemed.

Lan breathed in deeply, finding her resting heartrate had returned.

Of course. That was the reason why she couldn't stop the thoughts from hurtling through her brain. That was the reason why she'd come here in the first place.

So, resolving not to think any longer, she lay herself back down on the bench, raised her hands up and gripped onto the dumbbells once again. Today she felt a slight tightness in her biceps; the smallest sense that she might be on the brink of terrible injury; of terrible *pain*.

She paused for the shortest of moments, thinking this over; wondering if she shouldn't just shower herself off; get ready for her next shift. But then, feeling her heartbeat becoming steady once more, and her thoughts returning, she tipped the dumbbells off their spotter stand and went about the last part of her workout with a renewed vigour.

She wouldn't let anything stop her.

Not even her own body.

PROBATIONAL PERIOD

*N**ow dressed* in her stark, black overalls—those which were worn by members of the Security Division—Lan snapped shut the steel door of her locker located in Security HQ. As she did so, she couldn't help but catch a glance of herself in the mirror. She noted her tightly bound plaits; one hanging down at either side of her head. And she also noted her name; sewn onto the breast pocket of her overalls—L. NIU—just beneath the Chinese flag.

It brought a certain sadness to her every time she took in her appearance. It seemed almost as if she was some sort of a shadow rendition of her parents' expectation for her.

How they would have *loved* to have seen the ROCAF emblem sewn onto her breast pocket in place of her national flag . . .

Feeling a brain fog beginning to swamp down over her thoughts once again, she put the mirror image out of her mind, and turned her attention to the day's work ahead.

As she climbed the stairs into the main offices, she remarked to herself how it still felt strange not to have the familiar weight of a blaster pistol strapped to her thigh.

Of course she felt like a complete idiot after what had happened a few weeks ago; when she had somehow managed to shoot the very person she'd been supposed to protect—left him in the Infirmary. And the fact that it had been Gofreddo Zito only made matters worse.

Gofreddo Zito was the son of Costantino Zito; the creator of the Zito Entertainment Unit—the ZEU . . . or as it was just as often referred to, simply the 'Zito'.

Gofreddo Zito had gone out of his way in an attempt to make things easier for her. She knew that he had even spoken to her direct boss; head of the Security Division: Supervisor William Duval.

From gossip, she had heard that, following recovery from his injuries, Zito had turned up at Security HQ and effectively locked himself in Supervisor Duval's office for the best part of an hour; apparently explaining that it hadn't been Lan's fault.

But, as Lan knew, being a member of the Security team herself, there was a heavy dependence on trust. And once that trust had been breached, it was extremely difficult for it to be mended. Often, as Lan had found out during her time on Earth—when she had worked various private security positions around the globe— the employee who had made the mistake usually ended up leaving that particular job.

They just couldn't put up with the cold shoulder they were given by their fellow team members.

Obviously, the current situation was made all the more difficult because Lan happened to be currently working up on the Moon. It wasn't a simple matter of not turning up to work the next day and then hopping on the next transport out of town.

Then again, she had always liked to believe that she had a thicker skin than most.

She had, after all, suffered that most painful of experiences in being rejected by her very own parents. Now that she had carved out a life for herself—if not shown her parents then shown *herself* that she could manage alone—she knew for a fact that she needed to fight her own battles; that the buck stopped with her. And she had no intention of running...

Once she was up in the offices, she eyed the various cubicles—none of them with walls any more substantial than elbow height. Screens seemingly appeared out of thin air on each desktop, and many of Lan's fellow Security team members were working away feverishly at whatever their current task happened to be.

With a sigh which startled the person in the cubicle alongside, Lan sank into the articulated chair provided and tapped three times on the desktop to signal for her own screen to make an appearance. While the screen went through its initiation rituals, she found herself gazing out through the windows; out across the lunar plains, and to the rest of the Celestial Stays Dome.

She absorbed the skyline; all of the attractions put in place for the exotic—and by 'exotic' she of course meant *wealthy*—tourists who made the lunar colony a feasible financial proposition.

The Crescent Gardens.

The Lunar Grand.

The Stellar Tide Casino.

And then, off toward the periphery of the Dome, she made out the Lunar Caverns, and then the Armstrong Archive—off to its side the Orbital Café; once administered by Alicia Brennan.

At the Dome entrance, there was Entry Clearance which incorporated the Airlock, the Rover Pool—the parking space for the vehicles which carried passengers out to the Landing Site. Then there was Initiation Protocol, through which every person—tourist or employee—passed on arrival to the Celestial Stays Dome.

A little way further along, there was the Shuttle Hanger; the place where Lan's gaze would often linger; thinking back to the day . . . to the day when she had made her Big Mistake in shooting Gofreddo Zito. The mistake which saw her sat at this desk and minus her sidearm.

She stared on at the Shuttle Hangar another few moments before returning to reality. She turned to the screen before her, and passed a gaze over her incoming messages; the ones which she had received while she had been on her break; while she had been working up a sweat in the gym.

There were the usual circulars—the Health and Safety bulletins from Human Resources.

There was a notice about a faulty piece of body armour which was to be returned immediately for exchange . . . this no longer applied to Lan, though, because she no longer *needed* a suit of body armour . . .

As she did every day, she skimmed the messages half wondering if she might have something there from her parents. She knew that after fifteen years—and with apparently as much effort on her part as that of her parents to stay in touch; which was to say *no effort at all*—it was nothing but wishful thinking that they would somehow send her something now.

There was, however, one message which stopped her dead in her tracks.

It was from her boss: Supervisor William Duval.

He wanted to see her in his office right now.

Feeling as if he might be watching her at this exact moment, Lan shifted a quick glance about the offices. But all she saw was diligently working *desk jockeys* . . . all the misfits of the Security team; those who had proven themselves unreliable in action, or had been deemed unfit on arrival.

All those who were only fit for sitting at a *desk* all day.

Lan took a deep breath, still feeling the strain in her muscles from the high-intensity workout she'd put herself through earlier. Then she rocked herself to her feet.

Supervisor Duval's office was the floor above the main offices.

Like the other offices assigned to Supervisors, windows occupied the walls, offering a 360-degree view of the surrounding area.

Duval himself was at his desk, a frown stretched across his mouth as he busied himself with the screen before him. Although he was—*at best*—in his late-forties, he was a hulk of a man.

He had great, big biceps, and his pectoral muscles seemed to refuse to be restricted by the confines of whatever item of clothing he chose to wear. It seemed that Security HQ's interior designers had neglected to bear someone of Duval's body shape in mind when they had realised their plans. It actually brought on a slight smile for Lan to think it, but she found herself unfavourably comparing Duval with an orangutan trying and failing to use human furniture.

Duval had silver hair and leathery skin. Like the other members of the Security Division—*like Lan*—he wore black overalls. His Supervisor's badge shimmered golden on his breast pocket while the red-and-white, maple-leaf of the Canadian flag was sewn onto the one opposite.

His name W. DUVAL was neatly and unambiguously stitched into the fabric of his overalls beneath the Canadian flag.

As Lan stepped closer, Duval remained absorbed by whatever it was he was doing with his screen. She knew, from experience, that it was better not to break Duval's concentration, especially when she was clearly on thin ice as it was.

When members of the Security team found themselves called to Duval's office, it normally wasn't for a hearty slap on the back.

Finally, Duval deigned to glance up from his desk.

He met her eye, pouting as he did so.

This was something which Lan had observed Duval do with any given member of his team, and Lan often secretly wondered if he might not have the ability to read minds. It was, of course, scientifically proven—over and over again—that such a thing was not possible . . . and yet she couldn't help but wonder.

Sometimes she was *certain* there was more to the world than met the eye.

That something lurked just beneath the surface.

The air smelled lightly of peanut butter, and Lan recalled how she had more than once caught Duval walking through the offices —some imperative matter clearly on his mind—a teaspoon with a dollop of peanut butter firmly wodged in-between his lips.

Duval drew in a deep breath then sighed it out, all over the screen before him. He waved his hand at the screen and it immediately vanished into thin air.

Lan felt somewhat uneasy, unsure whether Duval's obviously grumpy mood had to do with her or the screen.

Duval leaned back slightly in his chair, tilted his head to one side and squinted. "How long've you been on probation, Niu?"

Although Lan knew the precise time period right down to the minute, she decided to be tactful. Not to show him her hand right away. "About two weeks, sir."

Duval pouted again, then nodded to himself. He remained

silent for a couple of seconds, and Lan couldn't help but feel a note of uneasiness in the atmosphere. She wondered if she was somehow making Duval nervous; and, at the same time, she wondered just how that would be possible.

In all the time she had been acquainted with Duval, she had never known him to be anything but stolid . . . emotion*less* even.

"And," Duval said, finally continuing, "what would you say you've learned during this provisional period?"

Lan felt her stomach muscles tighten. " 'Learned', sir?"

"Hmm, yes." He paused again. "Do you feel that you're capable . . ." He seemed to search for the word a long while. "Do you feel that you're *in the right place* emotionally and psychologically?"

Here Lan felt her whole body stiffen. After the incident, she had been given several sessions of compulsory therapy in the Infirmary; apparently in the hope that she would get over the experience of having *shot* someone by accident. Even though there couldn't have been more than half a dozen sessions, Lan had already felt that her assigned therapist was wandering in some deeply uncomfortable places, and she had been very glad to finish with the sessions for good.

She wondered if this might be a dig on Duval's part; if he was subtly highlighting this fact, that Lan had decided against taking the optional extra sessions. To be honest, Lan hadn't seen the point of them . . . it wasn't like Gofreddo was the first person she'd ever shot, and—if she kept up with this whole security game—he was unlikely to be the last either.

"I've always admired you," Duval said, leaning back further in his chair, and making the joints squeak slightly. He nodded at her. "You stay in good shape—you know how to follow an order—and . . ." he left this final comment lingering before finishing ". . . you *aren't* afraid to take action." He smiled slightly; an expression which looked wildly out of place on Duval's face. "I like that in one of my team members; I like that *a lot*."

Lan held herself still, feeling as if she couldn't so much as breathe easily until Duval averted his gaze from her; until he turned his attention back to something else. Throughout her childhood she recalled how her parents had often ground home the fact that she needed to make it her priority to *disappear*; to be *part of the crowd*; to *downplay* her achievements so that she might stand out for her humility; for her modesty.

Attributes which the Air Force valued highly.

Attributes which'd been responsible for her parents' successful careers.

And yet Lan couldn't help wondering if it indeed was the right thing for her to do.

If she had been one of her parents right now, she knew that she would've pressed her lips tightly together, and stared at a spot in mid-air.

But she *wasn't* either one of her parents.

Instead, she turned her gaze directly onto Duval. "Permission to speak frankly, sir?"

Duval cocked his head to one side, stretched his shoulders out, then said, "Go on."

Lan drew a biting breath in through her teeth. "Sir," she said, feeling that if she allowed her voice to shift from its affected gruff tone she would lose her nerve, "if I have to spend another day at *that* desk, flipping through *files* and *reports* and stuff like it; then I'm going to go crazy."

Even as she spoke the words, she realised how 'frankly' she was indeed speaking.

She wondered if she might not just be getting herself into more trouble.

Duval broke into a full-on, shit-eating grin. "Okey doke," he replied. "Hearing *that* message loud and clear."

Although Lan heard the enthusiasm—the *warmth*—in his voice, she couldn't allow herself to get carried away. And she absolutely could not allow herself to *relax*.

"So," Duval said. "What'd you recommend?"

"What do *I* recommend?"

"Uh-huh."

Lan thought about it for a moment, then she glanced out the window.

To the Shuttle Hangar.

When she turned back to Duval, he seemed to be performing that mind-reading trick of his again. "You wanna go back, huh?" he said. "Go back to the place it happened?"

"I think it's the best way to test whether or not I'm over it, sir."

Duval clenched a fist and brought his knuckles up to his lips. He gave his index-finger knuckle a couple of sucks then brought it away from his mouth. "And if it turns out you're *not*?"

Lan felt a skitter pass up her spine. She knew that she'd made a big mistake there; that she had presented a degree of vulnerability; a lack of confidence. And now it was too late for her to take it back. She pushed down the feeling, told herself to stay focussed.

"I *am* over it, sir." She looked him square in the eye. "I *promise*."

Duval continued to meet her eye for several more moments then he gave a stern nod. "All right, then," he replied. "I'll take your word for it." He glanced out the window, across the Celestial Stays Dome. "As it so happens, we've got an assignment at the Shuttle Hangar that's just rolled in." Again he broke into a smile. "In fact, if you hadn't brought up the matter yourself then I would've done so."

For the first time in their encounter, Lan allowed herself to relax slightly.

It felt as if the air had completely thawed now.

"Orders are on the Link—just consult and obey; nothing more."

With that, Duval turned his attention back to his desk, summoning the screen from thin air once again. As he sat there in the same—clearly uncomfortable; hunched-over pose—something tickled the base of Lan's gut.

"Sir?" she said, before she could stop herself.

Duval glanced up.

"Thank you for this opportunity—I won't let you down."

Duval gave her another firm smile, then a salute, before turning back to the screen on the desk before him.

Lan lingered another second more—just to savour the feeling—before turning on her heel and returning the way she'd come.

She only allowed herself to smile when she'd reached the bottom of the stairs.

She was back.

Back on patrol.

3

HUMAN-IMPLEMENTED
INEFFICIENCY

y some quirk of the system, when Lan checked in with the Link, using her neural implant, she found that she wouldn't be required to report for duty at the Shuttle Hangar until later in the day. As the Link informed her, she had four hours to fill as she wished.

Finding now that the laser-blaster compartment of her locker had been unsecured, she had toyed with the idea of going down to the shooting range; getting in some practice before the evening ahead. Although it had only been two weeks since she'd had her weapon confiscated, it felt a lifetime ago when she had last fired a laser blaster.

Despite her confident claim to Duval, that she was certainly ready for action, she had to admit that she felt something approaching a *skitter* through her veins to think about holding the laser blaster all over again.

What if she made another mistake?

What if she *shot* someone else?

That surely would be the end; a one-way ticket to her sitting on a desk till the end of her current rotation. And when she returned to Earth there would be little chance of her being considered for another rotation. It would be back to accepting low-level security positions; being a gun-for-hire . . . though that particular job description made what lay in store for her sound *far* more exciting than the reality would surely prove to be.

On balance, Lan decided to leave the laser blaster behind in her locker. And to head to the gym for another session before her shift later on in the day. It was better for her to take things slow; for her to take it 'one day at a time' . . . that was one of the phrases the therapist had somehow managed to gnaw into her brain by means of mind-numbing rote repetition at the beginning and end of each session.

Lan had hardly made it down to her apartment within the Basements—where she was planning on changing out of her Security overalls and putting on her gym kit—when she heard a familiar voice coming from behind her.

"Lan? Lan?"

Lan turned around.

She found herself nose to nose with Louise Williams; a Guardian who worked in the Crescent Gardens. Although Lan and Louise weren't what Lan would consider 'friends'—Lan wouldn't really consider that anybody in the world was her 'friend'—they had, what Lan had come to term, an easy acquaintanceship.

"Hey," Lan replied.

Like all other Celestial Stays employees—the ones who *didn't* work in the Security Division—Louise was dressed in royal-blue overalls. Her silver Guardian's patch sewn onto the breast pocket of her overalls glittered in the sharp fluorescent corridor light.

Her blond hair was swept back with an Alice band.

As always, or so it seemed to Lan, Louise had a healthy rosy-red glow to her cheeks.

"Skipping off work, too, huh?" Louise asked.

Although the comment was meant to be light-hearted, Lan couldn't help but feel a touch slighted by it. She didn't like it when anybody insinuated that she was anything less than a professional; that she was anything less than a highly skilled member of the Security Division.

At least when she wasn't going around shooting people who weren't supposed to be shot at.

"I . . . don't start until later," Lan replied.

Louise smiled lightly. "The night shift, huh?"

Lan looked beyond Louise, to the corridor ahead. To her room awaiting her, and the gym which was awaiting her beyond that. It was also part of her philosophy that—being a professional member of the Security Division—any employee of Celestial Stays could potentially become a target at any given moment. For this reason, it was better to stay on clean, cold terms with everyone.

"Yeah," Lan finally answered. "The night shift."

Louise seemed to notice Lan's impatience. When she spoke again, her voice was hurried, as if she was afraid that Lan might walk away if she went on for too long. "We were just wondering, you know, if you'd be interested in coming to a picnic tomorrow night."

"A 'picnic'?"

Louise nodded in reply, with a slight smile, and Lan wondered if she was already regretting having made the offer. "We're going to have it in the Crescent Gardens; just a small group of us . . . no more than a dozen."

For a couple of moments, Lan's mind froze.

She spoke without considering her words.

"And what made you think of me?"

Louise hesitated, then she glanced back along the corridor as if there was someone else she'd much rather talk to coming into view. "Oh, you know," Louise replied, her voice slightly floaty. "We just wanted to invite people around the Basements; we thought it'd be a good opportunity to get to know one another better . . ."

As Louise's voice trailed off, Lan felt her stomach sink slightly.

She had gone through her life alienating people, somehow managing to rub people up the wrong way. She noticed the effect she had on people every day of her life; how, when she walked into a room, if anyone was smiling or—*God help them*—laughing, they would take one look at her and stop. She realised that she had turned into something like a cartoon character; and not in a good way. If this had been a blockbuster film then she would surely have been the villain . . . or one of the villain's minions . . . And she didn't want to be that way any longer.

She didn't want to be *alone* any longer.

Louise parted her lips, apparently ready to say something else; ready to make some excuse so that she could leave Lan's—*apparently*—poisonous company.

But Lan was too quick for her.

"That sounds . . . *nice*," Lan said.

Louise seemed just as surprised as Lan at the words which'd tumbled out through her lips. But Louise managed not to look too shocked; she even managed to raise a smile. "Great," Louise said, then, moving off, "Look forward to seeing you there—I'll send you the info over the Link."

Lan watched Louise vanish around the corner, and then stood in surprise for a few seconds; surprised at *herself* . . . at the fact that she was acting somewhere near the realms of an ordinary human being.

4

MISTAKES REITERATED

*L*an *stepped out* of the PEAR—the Personal Transporter; the semi-automated vehicles which provided the transport infrastructure within the Celestial Stays Dome.

She listened to the PEAR's visor winding back downward, and trod her way along the path leading to the Shuttle Hangar.

Even just being here—standing before the building—she realised that she felt utterly different to how she had felt back in Duval's office.

Although she had hardly felt brimming with confidence as she stood before Supervisor Duval, she had at least had the nerve—had the *strength*—to be able to get the words out without her voice shaking all over the place.

Now, though, it wasn't just her voice she was worried about; her whole body seemed to be wracked with a trembling sensation. Just to take in the sight of the Shuttle Hangar; to know that the mistake she had committed had been *in there*.

The weight of the blaster pistol strapped to her thigh felt reassuring—as if she was in some way back to how things had been before the incident. And yet she knew that she could *never* go back. Even though Duval had undoubtedly said some kind things about her—words to the end that he *valued* her—she and Duval both knew that this was her last chance.

If anything went wrong this time, she was toast.

She'd be behind a desk for the remainder of her rotation.

That simple realisation seemed to give her a kick direct in the stomach. She supposed that someone experiencing the sensation could go one of two ways. They could crumple up into a nervous heap, or they could just *get on with it* . . . harness the nervous energy to drive them toward their goals; toward the completion of their day's work.

Strangely, Lan felt much better by the time she'd passed through the security doors and she stood in the hangar itself. It was strange because this was the place where she had taken the shot; where, in an attempt to protect Gofreddo Zito by firing at Alicia Brennan, she had instead shot him . . . or, perhaps, as went one account, he had jumped into the firing line.

Either way, that was no excuse.

When a person fires on another *unarmed* person then there can only ever be one who is in the wrong. And, this time, at least, it was *Lan.*

Lan cast her gaze over the Shuttles.

Down below, she could make out a pair of pilots speaking among themselves.

One of them had his back turned to her, while she could clearly make out the face of the other. It was Zito. Gofreddo Zito. The man she'd shot.

Lan fell into a daze. A tingling sensation passed across the surface of her skin; it brought out an array of goose pimples. Her heart hummed in her throat until she swallowed it down.

There was a moment when their eyes met.

When Lan peered into those sky-blue eyes.

His blond hair, as always, stuck up in all-over-the-place tufts.

Although she knew it was clearly an impossibility, she couldn't help picturing Gofreddo in her mind, his head stuck out the window of his Shuttle, feeling the lunar breeze blowing back his hair.

He squinted in her direction, as if he was having trouble confirming just who she was—that she was, indeed, the one who'd shot him. Finally, and this really did take Lan by surprise, he beckoned her over. Lan stood still, dumbstruck for a second or so.

And then she relented.

She took care going down the stairs, alert to her mental state, that she wasn't thinking at all clearly. It really would make her look something like an idiot if she tripped and fell with these two pilots standing by; watching on.

When she was back at ground level, she felt more secure; as if the lunar surface beneath her feet was more substantial. She had regained her sense of balance; her sense of solidity.

Gofreddo grinned and then nodded downward, at her thigh; to the blaster pistol she wore in the holster. "I was wondering when I would see you again. Back on duty."

"Yes, well," Lan replied, flicking a polite glance to Gofreddo's companion, before looking back to Gofreddo, "I suppose that I cannot be punished forever."

"No," Gofreddo said, "I suppose not." He turned and looked to his companion; the one who Lan hadn't really bothered to take in with any degree of depth.

But Lan did take him in now.

He had strawberry-blond hair.

Slight, curved features.

And a rounded chin.

He wasn't especially tall, but—*from Lan's expert eye*—she could tell that he had tight muscles beneath his overalls.

Her pulse quickened.

And her whole body went rigid, highlighting the soreness in the muscles she'd been working so hard throughout that day.

She glanced to his overalls—to the Guardian's badge—and then to the sewn-on name on the opposing breast pocket:

P. FOURIE

The flag—Lan instantly recognised—belonged to the Republic of South Africa.

She recalled that at some stage in her childhood—probably during some of the many countless hours she'd spent with the Cadets—she had memorised every flag in the world.

It wasn't as hard as it sounded.

Give or take, two hundred designs.

It took Lan a couple of seconds to realise that Gofreddo's companion—*P. FOURIE*—had spoken to her. Only when she glanced down, saw that he extended his hand out toward her, did she remember herself. She might be what she'd overheard an ex-colleague refer to as an 'Ice Queen', but she wasn't about to step on a common courtesy.

She took his hand.

Shook it.

His grip was strong.

No-nonsense.

Despite his ear-to-ear grin, and the sparkle glinting at the corners of his hazel eyes.

"Name's Patrick Fourie," he said, with an unmistakable South-

African lilt to his accent. He nodded to her. "That's some hair you've got there; guess it goes all the way down your back when you let it free, huh?"

Lan felt herself taken aback for a moment. It was—*all at once*—a self-conscious and a deeply reactive gesture to reach back and stroke the plaits she had woven into her hair that morning. Her hair had always been long, even when she'd been in the Cadets. That had always been a point of dispute with her mother, and they had come to an uneasy agreement that when Lan joined the ROCAF she would be required to cut it short.

However, the way things had panned out had allowed Lan to keep it long.

Despite this, though, she had always felt self-conscious about her appearance; had always been deeply aware of her whole body. And her hair was no different. Why she hadn't taken the decision to cut her hair shorter—so that she'd be able to better blend into the background, wherever she might be—escaped her somewhat.

Lan realised that Patrick Fourie—*Guardian Fourie*—was continuing to stare at her, waiting for her to answer what he no doubt believed to be a light 'quip'.

She felt strangely nervous when she met his eye. And her voice nearly shook as she replied. "It reaches my hip," she said, and then, realising that she hadn't reciprocated with her own name, added, "Lan Niu; pleased to meet you."

Guardian Fourie pouted, and then shifted a sidelong glance at Gofreddo Zito.

Gofreddo Zito himself was grinning.

If Gofreddo Zito was attempting to put Lan at ease then he wasn't being all that successful.

There was something about friendliness—particularly when it was directed at herself—which took Lan off-guard.

"So," Gofreddo Zito put in, finally breaking the slightly frosty silence which'd grown between the three of them, "we've got about an hour before the guests show up for the standard tour; do you think you're up to a little Shuttle run? Give your guts a chance to become used to the *extreme* speed?" Here Gofreddo shifted a glance at Guardian Fourie. Looking back at Lan, he said, "What'd you say?"

Lan managed to regain something of her natural gritty determination. "I'm sure I can handle it."

When she turned to Guardian Fourie, she saw that he was smiling widely, as if he was sharing some private joke with Gofreddo Zito. "The last member of the Security Division who said that lost their lunch about a klick out from the Dome."

Despite the swagger—the poorly disguised sense of arrogance in Guardian Fourie's voice—Lan couldn't help but feel the tightening, twisting sensation in her gut.

She was determined not to be *anything* like the 'last member of the Security Division'.

5

IN-FLIGHT SCHEMATICS

*L**an felt the shoulder harnesses* digging deeply into her skin. They came down across her chest, seemingly choking the air from her lungs faster than she could breathe it in. But there was none of the nausea, despite the constant aerobatics which Gofreddo Zito—sat at the controls—was performing.

As they went through with yet another barrel roll, ending with a sharp ascent followed by a sudden drop and levelling out, Lan managed to get a better look at Guardian Fourie. She read the smile lines deeply entrenched on his face. He was clearly having the time of his life; flying along here at who-knew-what velocity with his very best buddy.

The two of them trying to scare the wits out of their 'green' passenger.

Well, if that was indeed their goal, then they had failed.

Because Lan wasn't afraid.

Back in the Cadets, she had ridden through all manner of aerobatics, and at all different sorts of speeds and altitudes. She had even flown gliders solo herself, for a time.

No, if they really wanted to put the scare up her then they would have to work a little harder. They would have to put more imagination into their efforts.

As Gofreddo Zito levelled out the Shuttle, Lan took stock of the Lunar One Monument passing by beneath them. She couldn't help but notice the somewhat wistful glance which Gofreddo Zito cast out through the pilot's window. Of course, just like everyone else, she knew the news; about how Gofreddo Zito's grandfather had perished in the Lunar One mission; and how, more recently, his grandmother had flown to the Moon so that she might be buried beside her late husband.

Everybody had seemed to have an opinion on the event; opinions which ranged from the sentimental to something like *outrage* at the political implications.

Because, as the rules and regulations governing the Moon stated, human beings were not permitted to be interred beneath the lunar surface.

The Lunar One disaster had, of course, been a far different set of circumstances; taking place before the colonisation of the Moon.

Now, though, every year there were more and more efforts— taken on behalf of Earth governments—to bring a tighter rule to the Wild West of the Moon.

Gofreddo Zito continued to eye the Lunar One memorial before breaking off his gaze and turning back to the lunar surface out ahead. She noted that he had changed course now; that he was headed for the Celestial Stays Dome.

As they trundled their way over the lunar surface, Lan noted the slightly more sombre tone which lingered within the Shuttle—she supposed that Guardian Fourie was familiar with Gofreddo Zito's sudden mood shifts; that passing in close proximity to the Lunar One Monument—where his grandfather and grandmother were buried—tended to turn him into being more reflective; more introspective.

When they arrived at the Shuttle Hangar, the guests were waiting for them.

Each and every one of them wore the burgundy Celestial Stays overalls—the ones which were specially assigned to paying guests; tourists. There was about a dozen or so of them, and their ages ranged from, what Lan guessed to be, six to sixty. An entire family.

From their complexions, and the way that the few women among them wore headscarves in addition to their burgundy overalls, she took them to be Middle-Eastern in origin.

Being a member of the Security Division, Lan spent a large amount of her time standing and observing. Although she'd never have thought to remark on something like it back on Earth, she'd grown accustomed to the multi-cultural, international feel to the Celestial Stays workforce.

Whenever she returned to the Basements—the employees' residences—it was unlikely that, when she glanced across a crowd—say in the cafeteria—she would see anything other than a wide array of races and cultures; all of them eating together; all of them *socialising* together.

It was entirely different, though, when it came to the guests.

When it came to the lunar *tourists*.

They would, almost without exception, arrive in mono-racial, mono-cultural groups. This wasn't *all* that surprising, of course, given that tourists undertaking such a trip would mostly choose to take it with their loved ones; with their family members.

All the same, it still struck Lan as odd to see so many people of the same race—of the same *culture*—all bundled together into a single group.

Maybe those two weeks working behind a desk at Security HQ had taken a larger toll on her than she had imagined; this *was* her first interaction with tourists for that length of time.

It was a standard Lunar Shuttle outing, which was to say that Gofreddo Zito—with Guardian Fourie in the co-pilot's seat—guided them across the lunar plains; notably leaving out the aerobatics. Lan was along in accordance with procedure.

Even though it seemed innately unlikely that any member of this family unit would cause trouble, she was required to be on hand in case her laser blaster might be needed.

It was no joke to take a group of people out in a Lunar Shuttle; especially when it came to endangering the pilot's safety. Simply put, if anything became of the pilot, and the co-pilot, it might prove impossible to return to the Dome.

At least not without crashing the Shuttle into the lunar surface.

Once they'd gone through with the tour—everything going to plan—Lan realised that she was beginning to feel more comfortable with the whole experience; that she was feeling better about being back on the job. About being *out* from behind the desk.

It was only as they were returning to the Dome that Lan noticed something.

One of the family members—one of the children; a boy of about six, as she estimated—had come loose from his shoulder straps. He was now walking freely about the Shuttle; his parents, uncles, aunts, grandparents—other potential carers—otherwise occupied.

Even as Lan eased out from her shoulder straps, she acknowledged that it wasn't a difficult scenario to foresee. After all, it wasn't every day that you took a trip across the lunar surface.

There *was* a lot to see.

The Earth far above; a blue-and-white giant dominating the sky.

Endless space stretching out all around.

Stars dotting the heavens.

As the child threatened to slip in-between the pilot and co-pilot's seats—and to arrive too close to comfort to the controls there—Lan intercepted him; taking him with a gentle but firm grip under his arms. With the boy tilting his head back to examine her, no doubt confused about this turn of events, she brought him back to her own seat, and sat him down on her knee; pulling her shoulder straps down over her body with practised grace.

They arrived back to the Dome without any further incident.

Settling down in the Shuttle Hangar.

Lan looked on with a wry smile as the boy's parents suddenly realised that he'd gone missing and began to glance frantically about, as if he might've somehow—*soundlessly*—slipped out of an airlock and drifted down to the lunar surface.

When the gaze of the woman Lan took to be the boy's mother crossed her own, the entire family turned to look in her direction. Again, Lan felt self-conscious. She blushed heavily.

The woman thanked her many times over, scolding herself as she smiled at Lan, taking the boy from her.

Lan remained in her seat as each and every one of the family members bent down to shake her hand for the apparently good job she had performed. She watched the guests off the Shuttle, down the steps, and back out of the Shuttle Hangar; already being taken beneath the wing of the grinning member of the Hospitality Division assigned to them.

Now that it was only Gofreddo Zito, Guardian Fourie and herself alone in the Shuttle, Lan couldn't help but feel extremely tense. She knew that there was an argument to be made that she had broken with protocol; that, like any other passenger, she should technically have remained seated unless otherwise instructed by the pilot.

But she had acted on impulse.

Hadn't that been one of the qualities which Duval had claimed he most admired in her?

One of the qualities he most *valued* in her?

Gofreddo Zito said nothing about the incident as he passed her by, pausing only to lean into her and give her a wink, muttering a barely audible, "Good job" as he slipped off the Shuttle.

It left Lan alone with Guardian Fourie.

And Lan couldn't help but feel nervous in his presence.

That it was only the two of them.

Getting up from his seat, Guardian Fourie said, "They're sharp eyes you've got there, Niu."

It sent a slight tingle through her blood just to hear him utter her surname.

Guardian Fourie continued, "Should've been my job—to keep tabs on anyone who might get loose during the flight." He gave himself a mock slap on the cheek, and Lan couldn't help wondering if he was lightly making fun of her, or if he was attempting to hide a deeper sense of shame at having neglected his duty. Whatever he felt, he kept up his easy smile. "We live and learn, eh? Good thing we had a safe pair of hands such as yours about the place."

Lan really had no idea what came over her.

Perhaps it was the same sense of impulse which'd forced her up and out of her seat and to that child's aid. Maybe some part of her felt that if she was only to follow her gut it would lead her to fulfilment and happiness. She eyed Fourie, then said, "Guardian, are you busy tomorrow night?"

This brought on a look of curiosity in Guardian Fourie; soon followed by a look of confusion. "Patrick," he said. "*Please.*"

Lan couldn't help thinking that she'd made a big mistake.

One which she wouldn't be easily able to rectify.

What *had* she been thinking?

"Uh," Guardian Fourie—*Patrick*—replied, "I don't think so . . . why?"

Lan wished the ground would swallow her up.

That she might simply disappear.

And only wishes could save her now; or so it seemed.

She knew she had to go on, or risk looking even more ridiculous.

"There's a picnic . . . in the Crescent Gardens . . . just some . . ." she faltered for a long second before deciding there was no other option but to use the word ". . . *friends.*"

The proposition seemed to dawn on Fourie gradually.

Finally, he shrugged his shoulders, gave a slight frown. "Actually," he said, "I think I might be tied up." He closed one eye and narrowed the lid of the other one as if he was attempting to make out something in more detail. "Maybe another day?"

"Oh, uh . . ." Lan replied, feeling strangely numb. "Sure."

Patrick's features softened slightly and he nodded firmly. "See you around," he said, as he walked toward the Shuttle exit.

And, just like that, Lan was all alone.

All alone with her *idiocy.*

6

UNORGANISED MAMMALIAN
WONDERINGS

*P*atrick *Fourie trod away* from the Shuttle, and away
from that delightful creature; Lan Niu . . . *Lan.*

He knew that it was going to be extremely difficult to get his
mind shot of that delicate, pale skin; and the tight, well-muscled
throat which'd been visible above the neckline of her jet-black
Security overalls. And *that* hair; he longed to unravel those plaits,
and to comb his fingers through it. To lose himself in it. To see just
how long it *really* was.

He was still reeling from their meeting in the Shuttle; when
they'd been alone.

He had been playing it cool, of course.

Although he'd hardly have described himself as any sort of *Don
Juan*, he knew all about the importance of being *inaccessible* . . . of
making himself *unattainable.*

Sure, that was the line of logic he *liked* to believe he had
followed in rebuffing her invitation, but, in truth, he knew that it

was merely because she had caught him by surprise. He hadn't been expecting anything like that; for Lan to be so direct with him.

A woman like that could have her pick of the men beneath the Celestial Stays Dome.

Until recently Patrick had been more or less certain that any women who hung around him were there because they wanted to get closer to his best friend Gofreddo. They all wanted to use Patrick as some sort of a shortcut to the world-renowned, millionaire playboy. It was a wonder that he ever managed to make himself genuinely believe that any of those girls would be interested in a poor rancher's son from Durban, South Africa.

He had never been particularly tall, but he had always done the best with what he had. Of course, it had helped his goal that he *had* grown up a rancher's son, because the nature of the work meant that he had developed natural, 'working muscles'—as his father termed them.

Whenever he had had girlfriends—the few that there had been —it was due to him putting in the 'grunt work' . . . him doing his *damndest* to have them take notice of him.

And that was why it was so surprising that this girl—*this beauty!* —had come right out and propositioned him so directly.

Already he was regretting his response.

Allowing his indecision—his *surprise*—to show through so easily.

When Patrick reached the locker rooms, something struck him —the feeling that he simply *had* to turn back; that he needed to return to the Shuttle Hangar.

And so he did.

But, amongst the warm, reassuring smells of grease and oil, he realised that Lan Niu had already disappeared. She had escaped him.

He allowed himself a profound breath, and then screwed up his features in frustration.

He only managed to draw himself back from despair by reasoning with himself that he had told her to suggest a different time or place.

But would she really have taken it like that?

Hadn't it come across as an obvious brush-off?

Patrick just didn't know any longer.

He didn't know *what* to think.

Well, one thing was for certain, he wouldn't be able to do anything about it now; he had to bide his time; wait the whole thing out.

Be patient.

As Patrick turned his back on the Shuttle, returning to the locker rooms to go change into his mechanic's overalls, he allowed himself a sly smile.

If there was anything in this world he was good at—*anything at all*—it was being patient. There wasn't much he could learn about patience that he hadn't learned while lying back in the long grasses, beneath the old, treasured, Ana tree, counting the fluffy clouds blowing their way leisurely past; dreaming about what his life might have in store for him beyond the endless wooden fences of the ranch, and the stench of horse sweat in the height of the summer months.

He could be patient; of that there was little doubt.

7

ORGANIC UPKEEP

*L*an gripped the handlebars of the static bicycle tightly. She flurried her legs on the pedals, feeling the high resistance she'd selected bringing a soreness out in her thighs and calves. She channelled the whole force of her body down through her legs. Through her earpiece, her neural implant informed her that she had just hit the twenty-kilometre mark. It reminded her of the current amount of calories she'd burned, as well as advising her of her speed. As a kind of aside, it informed her that she had just set a new maximum velocity.

Lan hardly noticed the data, though, she had never been all that much interested in data; she was more interested in the sensation of exercise itself, and its effect on her brain.

How it just made everything go away.

How it seemed to cause her to regress into some sub-human state.

A state in which she didn't need to live in this world any longer.

Lan had always been a non-drinker, and she often wondered if the addictive urges she felt toward exercise—the desperate desire for escape—might've manifested themselves in some form of substance abuse. She recalled, through some of the forced therapy sessions following her shooting of Gofreddo Zito, that the therapist had asked her about her exercising 'ritual'—the therapist's word, not Lan's. And Lan had just fobbed her off with some bullshit excuse.

She didn't see why she had to share anything about her life . . . because, well, it was *her* life.

Feeling that her breathing was coming heavier—that she was beginning to *puff*—she reduced the force of her pedalling. She lowered herself back down onto the saddle of the static bike. She perched there for a few seconds, continuing to pedal away with about half the resistance she had set before. Then she stop pedalling completely.

Legs aching, and her body trembling slightly from the ordeal she'd put it through, she reached down for the towel she'd brought along with her; and which she'd allowed to fall to the floor when she'd mounted the bike.

Her mother had always gone on about how she was 'careless' when it came to organising herself; when it came to tidying up after herself.

Lan's bedroom at home had been in constant disorder.

Her room in the Basements was now in a similar state.

For some reason, Lan could never suck up the requisite motivation to clean her room. She liked to make the places she stayed seem 'lived in' . . . was that a crime?

Lan pressed the towel to her face, wiping the sweat from her skin. Then she reached out for the water bottle she had left perched up against the static bike frame. She brought the bottle to her lips and drank deeply. The water had something of a restorative effect on her. She felt it plough down through her body like an elixir, removing the most urgent aches and pains, and seeming to cool her over-heated temperature. As she stood up, sucking on the bottle of water, she surveyed the gym.

It was much busier than it had been that morning.

Although she didn't bother to count, Lan was certain that there were more than two dozen Celestial Stays employees here. As she always did whenever she found herself facing off with a crowd, she skimmed faces, never settling too long lest someone realise she was looking at them; lest they look back *at her*.

When Lan continued her rotation, and reached the doorway to the gym, she stopped dead.

And she focussed in more closely.

It was Guardian Fourie.

Or *Patrick*, as he'd told her to address him.

Lan wasn't certain she'd be able to get her head around that.

Throughout her time with the Security Division, she had always stressed to herself the importance of reverence for her superiors; that she was not—*under any circumstances*—to lower herself to *informality* . . . to *casual* expression.

Before Lan could look away, she realised that she'd caught his eye. Although she switched her attention to the water bottle in her hand, and took a quick sip, she could *feel* his eyes passing over her. Not for the first time that day, she wished for the ability to disappear.

"Mind if I butt in?"

Lan turned around.

Realised that she was now standing nose to nose with Alicia Brennan—the woman who had put an end to Gofreddo Zito's womanising days. The woman who had cooked up *several* storms at the Orbital Café, and who was now Supervisor of Catering; based in the Lunar Grand Hotel. Like Lan, Alicia was dressed in a tracksuit; ready for her workout.

Lan found her voice a couple of heartbeats later. "Uh, sure, go ahead."

"Thanks," Alicia replied, giving her a wide smile and a couple of blinks.

A couple of blinks of her tangerine eyes which said—at least to Lan—that she was actively *trying* to be polite even though Lan was the one who'd shot her beau.

Mainly because she didn't want to suffer the humiliation of treading her way across the gym floor—and past Guardian Patrick Fourie—Lan allowed Alicia past and then didn't shift from her spot. She squeezed the bottle of water in her fist, listening to the *scrunch* of the plastic. Right when Lan was beginning to lose herself in her own thoughts, Alicia spoke up from her new position on the saddle of the exercise bike. "Which one is he?"

"Huh?" Lan replied, turning back to Alicia.

The two of them met eye to eye.

Lan felt her chest tighten.

Her heart fluttered in her throat.

A jolt of blood shot up to her temples.

Alicia, peddling gently on the static bike, but with her full attention fixed on Lan, said, "It's obvious—I can see it in your eyes." She removed a hand from the handlebar grip and waggled her finger at the tip of Lan's nose. "Deny it at your peril."

Almost despite herself, Lan felt a slight smile sneak onto her lips. "What makes you so certain?"

"Do you *dare* bring into question womanly intuition?"

Lan decided that she didn't . . .

Although Lan didn't know quite why, she remained on the same spot, looking out over the gym, taking stock of the tread-mills, the elliptical trainers, and the weights benches. Because she couldn't help herself, she mentally critiqued each weight-lifter's form and technique. Sometimes it made her smile to think that there were so many people who wanted to lift weights—to grow themselves big, bulging muscles—and yet couldn't be bothered to seek out professional assistance before they did so. At least chiro-practors would continue to have a steady stream of clients.

"Louise told you about the picnic, didn't she?"

Lan switched her attention back to Alicia.

Alicia was still very much in the saddle, and clearly not putting too much effort into her pedalling. It looked as if she'd gone out for the day in the park; going slowly enough so that she would be able to smell the flowers on her way.

Was this the reason why people didn't get along well with Lan?

Because she always thought this way?

Because she was *always* critical?

Lan tried her best to shut off that particular part of her mind.

And was mostly successful.

Lan nodded in reply to Alicia's question.

Alicia smiled broadly, then cocked her head to one side. "*So,*" she said, drawing out the syllable. "Who're you going to bring along?" She rolled her eyes up in their sockets, then added, "Don't tell me you're skittish about inviting someone, are you?"

Now Lan felt herself blushing.

The heat rising in her cheeks.

"Actually," Lan said, "I already asked someone."

Alicia stopped pedalling completely.

She removed both hands from the handlebars, then leaned into Lan. "*Who?*"

Lan swallowed hard, then looked across the gym. She realised that Patrick was no longer there. That he had gone off to get himself a shower; or something.

Or *something*.

Maybe he'd gone to meet a girlfriend of his.

That could be one explanation.

Lan glanced back to Alicia and decided she had nothing to lose. She should've been thankful that Alicia was so much as *looking* at her after Lan had nearly killed her boyfriend.

"It was Patrick," Lan said. "Patrick *Fourie*."

For a fraction of a second, Lan was certain that Alicia's eyes would clean pop right out of their sockets. That they would slip free and bounce down at their feet.

But, thankfully—if only for Alicia—they stayed put.

Alicia glanced around, then said, "I thought I saw him when I came in here. Goodness, and there's Fred, like always, not telling me *anything* . . . not even when it's his best friend." She rolled her eyes. "That's boys for you, huh?"

"Yeah," Lan replied, her voice damp; without any force.

Alicia turned her attention back to the exercise bike and began to peddle again. "We'll look forward to seeing you two, anyway." She shook her head, still smiling widely. "Goodness, who'd have known it, huh? *Patrick* . . . he always was a sly one."

Lan thought about telling Alicia the truth—about telling her that Patrick had turned her down, but Alicia looked so pleased with herself, and, beneath everything else, she didn't want to ruin the good mood she'd seemingly put her in. So she just left it there.

"Well," Lan said, clearing her throat, "I . . . guess I'll see you around?"

Alicia beamed at her, and then quickened her peddling. "I've got a mountain of cupcakes to burn off in the next hour—all this tasting just isn't good for a girl's hips."

Lan managed a slight smile then excused herself. As she left the gym behind, she was almost paralysed with fear that she'd run into Patrick on the way out.

And that he would humiliate her all over again.

8

TIMELY REMINDER

Reporting for duty the next day, Lan left the locker room at Safety HQ behind—her blaster pistol safely strapped to her thigh. After she'd checked with the Link that morning, she'd found that she'd been assigned to the Stellar Tide Casino for the day's shift. To be honest, despite no longer finding herself behind a desk—despite having been handed her freedom by Duval—she wasn't relishing the day's work. She still had the previous day's events etched deeply into her mind.

In particular the rejection by Patrick.

And then the sparking of a misunderstanding with Alicia.

It was a mess, and one which she would have to untangle sooner or later.

And *sooner* rather than later.

Lan set foot over the threshold of the Stellar Tide Casino. She began to hear the constant, jarring sounds of the slot machines; the rolling of the ball around the roulette; and the more subtle *snaps* of cards being slapped down on blackjack tables. She had never seen the attraction of gambling, but, then again, she'd never been in the financial position where she could see gambling as anything other than mortifying. She understood the fundamental principal; that those who had the money—or didn't, as the case might've been—wanted to feel a flush of excitement; the chance of improving their score; of leaving with more than they'd come in with.

But it was just like that old cliché she often heard bandied about with respect to gambling; casinos weren't built from the winners . . .

That said, Lan did her best not to judge anyone—none of the super-rich who inevitably made up the Celestial Stays clientele. She'd learned long ago that, where you were born—and who you were born to—really did matter in the real world. That had been a lesson she hadn't quite appreciated until she had struck out on her own; until she had left her parents' influence behind.

Until she had had the chance to *appreciate* her parents' influence.

The Stellar Tide Casino had been one of her most frequent spots on the beat. In some ways it was notorious . It was one of those locations which seemed to breed danger in and of itself . . . she certainly never let her guard down while she was on patrol here. Although she had never needed to draw her blaster pistol, she had certainly had somewhat unpleasant confrontations with gamblers who'd had a bad run of luck, and who were clearly coming close to violence with the dealers running the tables. She prided herself on her cool-headedness in those situations; how she believed that she could calm down even the most riled of gambler.

For some reason she still clung to that antiquated belief that men were essentially inclined to treat women differently; that they were much less likely to commit an act of violence against a woman.

At least out in public.

Perhaps if she believed otherwise she wouldn't have been able to do her job with such staunch, cool-headed detachment.

Lan stood her ground, assuming the position of appearing to be minding her own business while, in reality, she was keeping a very watchful eye on everything playing out before her.

Long ago, she had learn that being unperceived in any given location was the greatest of advantages for a security guard.

As she kept a subtle watch on everything occurring across the casino floor, she noticed a pair of familiar figures. There was Guardian Julius Denisov, the man in charge of the Stellar Tide Casino. Alongside him trod the Supervisor of the Human Resources Division, Mackenzie Angliss.

As Lan regarded them, she couldn't help thinking that they looked like an extremely odd pairing; that the two of them seemed *bizarre* in one another's company.

There was Mackenzie Angliss; with her famed, laser-green eyes, flowing red hair and tanned complexion. And then there was Julius Denisov; with his cool, Slavic features and pale skin. Of course Mackenzie wore a golden Supervisor's patch sewn onto her breast pocket while Julius had a silver Guardian's patch sewn onto his own.

From what Lan could tell, they were deep in an argument.

Of course, to the casual observer, what with their gentle smiles, and the words they mumbled under their breath, they seemed as if they were having some civil, staff-based exchange of views; nothing *hostile* about it. But, to the trained eye—to *Lan's* eye—she could tell that they were in the midst of a terrible quarrel. Indeed, as they drew close to her, she caught a couple of the words being passed between them.

"You know the regulations," Mackenzie said, with that lilting, slightly jolly tone, which Lan recognised to be an Australian accent. "Gambling is licensed *only* to take place on the premises; beneath the roof of the Stellar Tide. Is there any way I can make that clearer to you?"

"But, Supervisor, listen, please," Julius replied, in a much more measured—*stern*—Russian-inflected accent, "I was only going by the most important of all considerations; that Celestial Stays clientele must—*at all times*—have their every whim and desire fulfilled."

Mackenzie glanced up, catching Lan's eye for a fraction of a second.

Lan was certain that she was going to make some witty remark —something along the lines of asking if Lan wanted to take a photograph, or a video. But, in the end, she said nothing at all.

Mackenzie continued, speaking to Julius, "That's only the start of it. Just because you have a passageway through to the Lunar Caverns doesn't mean that we're insured to take guests *through* it . . . what if something had gone wrong? What if there'd been a cave-in?" She shook her head, her voice fading as they walked away from where Lan stood. "We'd have *all* been for it. Do you understand what I mean?"

Lan followed Julius and Mackenzie with her gaze as they turned the corner and disappeared through one of the many security doors on the ground floor of the Stellar Tide Casino. No doubt they were going to resume their conversation in the back corridors; in a more private setting.

Of course, Lan knew all about the passageway leading to the Lunar Caverns. That had been just about the first thing she had discovered—the first *secret* she had discovered—when she'd started her beat here. That was how Louise had managed to evade Security and reach the Lunar Caverns; how she had managed to track down her former lover, Alex Barn.

In fact, Lan had been the one to tell her where she needed to go.

She was somewhat surprised that, during the course of the investigation into the Alex Barn Matter, she hadn't been implicated at all. Perhaps it was because there had been a happy outcome.

If things had ended any differently, she was certain that she might've got herself into deep trouble.

Feeling cramp beginning to set into her feet, Lan curled her toes, hoping that she'd be able to mitigate the uncomfortable, crawling sensation passing across the surface of her skin.

It helped; just a little.

"Lan? Lan Niu?"

Lan's heart skipped.

She hadn't quite got past the idea that whenever someone called her name she might be in some sort of trouble. That she might be about to find herself on the first ship headed back to Earth. It was strange that she should feel so attached to the Moon. Although she was a long way from being supernaturally inclined— her parents had knocked away any inclination in *that* direction a long while ago—she couldn't help feeling that she had 'unfinished business' of a sort on Luna.

She wanted to get through her rotation for some imperceptible reason.

When Lan glanced up, she realised that it was Kyra Singh.

Lan took in her sleek, nutty-brown hair. She had it tucked into a bun. Her constant, wide-eyed gaze Lan knew to be a red herring when it came to judging her character. In fact, Kyra had most likely managed the nearly unachievable during the whole Gofreddo-Zito affair. She was more implicated in his suffering than Lan had been.

During the episode, it'd been revealed that Kyra was a journalist; leaking news about Gofreddo Zito's grandmother—and her plans to be buried alongside her husband at the Lunar One Monument. It had justly caused a large stir back on Earth; not least because, officially, no one was supposed to possess the right to burial on the Moon.

The most common line—in keeping with the media's general attitude to the whole Celestial Stays project—was that the Zitos shouldn't be garnered with special treatment simply because of who they were. Simply because of the money they *had*.

In Lan's opinion, the matter wasn't as clear-cut as all that.

Gofreddo Zito's father had, of course, been one of the victims of the Lunar One disaster—the first mission to colonise the Moon. And although Lan hadn't ever really been sentimental about anything, she couldn't help but feel a *touch* of sentiment about this.

There was something melodramatic about flying a lady to the Moon so that she might be buried alongside the one she had loved throughout life.

Lan shifted her attention away from the recent past, and back onto Kyra.

To be honest, Lan hadn't realised that Kyra even knew her name.

It seemed odd that they hadn't met with one another at an earlier juncture; after all, they had both been so tied up in the whole ordeal with Gofreddo Zito. And Gofreddo Zito had gone out of his way to see that the two of them would be equally pardoned. All the same—even knowing that she'd been the one to *shoot* Gofreddo—Lan couldn't help but wonder at just how Kyra had managed to remain on Luna after all those news reports she had filed back down on Earth.

"Can I have a word?" Kyra said, her tone hushed; her voice almost lost among the general ambience of the Stellar Tide Casino.

Lan glanced about her, wondering if she might be being monitored.

She was on—for want of a better word—*probation*.

Lan looked Kyra back in the eye, and then gave her a nod.

"All right," Kyra said. "This way."

Kyra seemed to follow a similar route to that which Julius and Mackenzie had gone along a matter of minutes earlier. Even as Lan went along with Kyra, she couldn't quite shift the thought that this was an extremely bad idea; that Kyra was no doubt about to get her involved in something which might greatly jeopardise her Celestial Stays career.

So why *was* Lan following her?

Was it curiosity?

Because Kyra had been slightly forceful?

. . . Or maybe it was just a new sense of freedom—of *not* being trapped behind a desk—of Lan being able to wander about as much as she wished.

There was nothing much distinctive about the back corridor of the Stellar Tide Casino, other than the fact that it seemed discreet; that it seemed a location where somebody hoping to avoid detection might hide out. Why was Kyra hoping to avoid detection?

Lan met Kyra's eye, feeling the blaster strapped to her thigh strangely heavy.

She decided to take the upper-hand.

"What is it?" Lan said.

Kyra glanced around, again with a great degree of suspicion to her movements. "There's something you should know," she said, her voice taking on that sweet, smoothed-corners tone which she recognised as an Indian accent.

Lan focussed in on Kyra. It was difficult to trust someone who had been so clearly outed as a mercenary journalist—a *reporter* . . . Gofreddo Zito had to be the *only* reason Kyra hadn't been unceremoniously tossed into the first ship headed off Luna.

"About what?" Lan replied.

Kyra gave a slight pout. Her eyes skimmed over Lan's and then seemed to pick out some indistinct location in the shadows surrounding them. "It's about your parents," she said.

Lan felt her heart thump hard in her ribcage. "*What* about my parents?"

"Listen," Kyra continued, turning back to Lan. "It's not right that we do this here—that we do this *now*."

A surge of blood pulsed into Lan's temples.

She felt a sudden snap of anger.

"Why? Why *not*? What is it about my parents? What did they *say*?"

Kyra only pressed her lips tightly together, squeezing all the blood from them momentarily. "They're fine," Kyra replied, then looked back across the corridor, as if she feared imminent discovery. "I can't say any more than that." She glanced back at Lan. "Can you disable your Link?"

Lan thought about what Kyra was saying.

Like everyone else beneath the Celestial Stays Dome—like everyone else down on *Earth*—Lan had a neural implant which connected her to the Link; to the central network at the heart of human civilisation. To ask her to switch it off was like telling her to stop breathing. There was a general assumption that anybody who had the ability to disable their connection to the Link was bound to be a tearaway . . . some sort of *untrustworthy* character.

But, having said that, like many others before her, Lan had come across the odd occasion when she felt the need to disable the Link; to not be witnessed doing something she viewed as being either illicit or illegal.

It didn't take her long.

In fact, Lan had only to stick her finger into her earpiece, and to think of a specific image, and she felt the Link depart her mind. It was an odd sensation; one which Lan likened to the feeling of being back in one of those gliders—or, perhaps more accurately, like flying a small, single-propped plane after cutting the engine. All the noise and vibrations which'd come from the engine disappeared in a moment. And all was silent. It was natural . . . *strange.*

Lan tried to shift her attention away from the sensation, and back onto Kyra.

Onto what she had to say.

"Are you busy tonight?" Kyra asked.

Lan thought about the picnic.

She had agreed to go when she'd spoken to Louise. But that was before she'd made a fool of herself by asking Patrick Fourie if he would attend with her; and then made an *even greater* fool of herself when she'd allowed the fact to slip that she was interested in Patrick to Alicia; insinuated that the two of them would be arriving together.

Lan thought about the question again, before answering promptly. "No," she said. "I'm not busy tonight—*I'm free.*"

"Good," Kyra said, with a slight smile. "There's a picnic—one I've been invited to . . ."

Already Lan felt her heart dropping down to her stomach.

Her mind ebbed in and out.

It seemed like a nightmare; and one from which she had zero hope of escape.

Lan had already channelled out from what it was Kyra had been saying. She had stopped paying attention ever since she had mentioned the picnic. Flipping the Link back online, she glanced to Kyra, gave a nod, and then said, "I'll see you there later."

9

ENCUMBERED PREPARATION

*P*atrick *rolled himself* out from beneath the Shuttle on a creeper. The wheels of the creeper made a series of sharp *squeaks* and he wondered if they could use oil too.

He slapped the can down beside him, making it *clunk* on the cemented floor.

He grabbed for a grubby rag lying nearby and wiped his hands clean.

Then he rocked himself up off the creeper.

He straightened and examined the Shuttle before him, seeing if there were any other obvious signs of damage; of neglected maintenance.

On the way in, during the previous voyage, he had noticed how the Shuttle had been trimming ever so slightly too close to starboard. As he had flown the Shuttle back into the Hangar, he had wondered why Gofreddo hadn't told him anything about the problem; it was one of those issues which, if not treated at the source, could quite easily get worse.

It wasn't like Gofreddo to miss such an obvious problem, but, then again, Gofreddo had hardly been himself over the past few days. Several times, Patrick had thought about bringing up the issue with him, but the right moment had never cropped up. Then again, Patrick had never been all that great with Man-to-Man Chats; back on his father's ranch emotions—in either males or females—had very much been considered *verboten*.

Why, Patrick could recall one afternoon when he'd returned from mucking out the stables to discover his mother silently sobbing to herself while she washed the dishes.

When Patrick had asked her what the matter was, she had only smiled, and, through the tears streaming down her face, said, "Nothing, dear."

And, being his father's son, Patrick had believed her.

It wasn't until about a month later that Patrick learned the news; that his grandfather—his mother's father—had passed away. And they hadn't been able to muster the money to get to Cape Town; where his grandfather had been living in state-assisted care.

Although Patrick never pried into the particulars of the matter, he could well imagine that his father had taken the cold decision that it wasn't worth the financial outlay for them to travel there. His father had always been ruthless in balancing the books. In weighing up each and every one of his life decisions as a series of profits and losses.

Patrick's grandfather's funeral had been no different.

Hearing footsteps and nearing voices, Patrick turned his attention to the entrance of the Hangar. He saw, almost immediately, that Alicia and Gofreddo were plodding in through the doorway. This would hardly be the time for Patrick to bring up the issue with the Shuttle. Even though Gofreddo was better about playing down his *machismo* than a lot of other Latin men Patrick had known, he knew that it would be another matter entirely to rip into him in front of his girl.

With a faint smile lining his lips, Patrick observed Gofreddo —*with his hulking, muscular frame; and his tufted blond hair*—and Alicia—*with her tangerine eyes; her close-cut brunette hair which sawed down the side of her face.* He had to admit that they looked a *couple.*

They seemed to *belong* together.

Sometimes Patrick wondered if something like True Love might exist in his future; or was that too wild of a step for him to make?

What even *was* True Love anyway?

Did it just mean two people remaining together despite all the problems which cropped up around them? Did it mean a relationship like that between his mother and father? He couldn't recall ever having witness them kissing or even hugging one another.

Was that *True Love?*

Whatever Patrick's conclusion, he couldn't help but think that he knew True Love when he saw it; and Gofreddo and Alicia, as an item, were most certainly *it.*

"*¿Qué haces?*" Gofreddo said, as he drew close to Patrick.

"Uh," Patrick said, stumbling to reply. "Just fixing up the Shuttle."

Although Patrick spoke both English and his native Afrikaans fluently, he didn't see himself as being talented when it came to languages. Those two languages, after all, came to him naturally. He didn't *think* at all when he spoke them. Throughout the large amount of time they'd spent together, Patrick had picked up several phrases from Gofreddo—from Gofreddo's native Spanish. And, Patrick was sure, especially when something went wrong, Gofreddo had picked up no small amount of Afrikaans invective. However, neither of them were anywhere close to being able to converse in either's native language; and so they stuck with English; the language of Celestial Stays as much as it was of the Earth. Alicia, though, Patrick knew, was fluent in Spanish, and this was her and Gofreddo's preferred mode of communication when they were alone together.

Gofreddo gave Patrick a wry grin, then slipped Alicia a side-long glance. "We were just heading off to go get ready for the picnic."

Patrick flashed his eyebrows. " 'The picnic' ?" he echoed, his mind still somewhat stuck on the state of the Shuttle, and how he was supposed to break such news to Gofreddo.

This time Alicia stepped in, wrinkling her brow slightly as she responded. "Didn't Louise tell you about the picnic. *Tonight? The Crescent Gardens?*"

Patrick pursed his lips, forcing himself to remember. It was quite possible that Louise might've told him something about a 'picnic', but he also realised that it was equally as likely that she'd been in the company of her own lover—Njhay—and, as a consequence, Patrick had been doing his level best to get away from their lovey-dovey ways as soon as possible.

Was there anything *more* uncomfortable than being in the company of two people who had no issue with PDAs?

Patrick scanned his mind for an excuse. Just thinking about it, there didn't seem to be much appealing about spending his evening in the company of said lovey-dovey couples. He would much rather spend his evening in the company of the Shuttles, here.

It didn't matter what delicious treats Alicia might have in mind.

Patrick prepared to deal a polite rejection, but before he could so much as part his lips Alicia beat him to the punch.

This time he couldn't help noticing that she was smiling.

From ear to ear.

One of those smiles which told him that she had some great gossip . . . or that she at least *thought* she had some great gossip.

"What about that smoky little number of yours? Surely she went into details when she told you about the picnic?"

Patrick was genuinely perplexed. "What 'smoky little number' ? And what *picnic?*"

Here he decided to just come clean about the whole thing.

He didn't like to be the confused party.

But it was right then that something slipped into place in his memory.

His mind flipped back to the previous night.

To that girl . . . to that member of the Security Division . . . to Lan Niu.

He blinked away to himself as he did a mental inventory of her appearance; as if he might've forgotten all about her already. That long hair, split into a pair of braids. That sleek, pale skin. And those black—*black*—eyes; the ones which, if he didn't take care, he might easily lose himself in forever.

Niu.

Lan *Niu.*

When Patrick shifted his attention back onto Alicia and Gofreddo, he realised that they were both grinning at him. That they were clearly enjoying this moment of confusion, or embarrassment, whatever they *perceived* this moment to be.

"We'll see you there, Pat," Gofreddo said, reaching out and grasping hold of Patrick's shoulder; giving it a squeeze which momentarily stopped any blood flowing.

Alicia gave him a wink as she turned her back on him.

Patrick remained stunned—staring at the two of them as they departed the Hangar.

It was only a few seconds later that Patrick realised he still held the soiled rag in his hands. He gave his skin a final wipe-down, tossed the rag off onto the floor where it'd once been, and then made for the showers.

He had a picnic to prepare for.

10

RENDEZVOUS IN THE PARK

ack in her room, in the Basements, Lan spent an inordinately long time staring at herself in the mirror. She wasn't sure what she should do with her hair; if she should undo the businesslike plaits; the ones which kept her hair out of the way during the workday.

To be quite honest, she had no idea what it was that Kyra had in mind.

Would the two of them simply meet at the Crescent Gardens then take off for some other place? Or would they wander amongst the crowds while they spoke?

Just how many people were *going* to this picnic, anyway?

. . . There was only one person who Lan could say for certain *wasn't* going to the picnic.

Finally decided, Lan reached up and combed out her plaits. She had time—*about an hour*—before she had to take the PEAR to the Crescent Gardens. That was all she needed.

She jumped into the shower and worked to wash her hair down

her back, bringing it straight and glossy with the selection of shampoos and conditioners she'd brought with her up from Earth.

When she was done showering, she felt like an entirely different person, standing with her towel wrapped about her waist, examining herself in the mirror. Her long black hair now dangling down about her hips.

Allowing her hair to grow long had been one of the first things she'd done after she'd left home. Her parents had never allowed her to grow her hair any longer than shoulder-length; and even that had been a battle. It was always acknowledged that once Lan was signed up for the ROCAF she would need to keep her hair cut to the regulation length.

Which was to say *short*.

It had taken Lan the best part of about five years for her hair to grow out to this length, and now that it had she had sworn to herself that she would never get it cut again.

She was proud to absorb her pale, muscular body. To see the tight biceps and triceps. The flat, rippling stomach. The powerful, cable-like legs.

She recalled the first time she had begun to work out she had worried that she might lose her female form; that she might become either curveless, or deformed by burgeoning muscles. She realised that those had only been the concerns of her mother; the ones which might drive off male attention . . . which might make her 'less attractive'.

Well, Lan didn't know an awful lot about male attention—let alone male *attraction*—but what she did know was that she caught them looking from time to time.

Actually, to tell the truth, more than just *time to time* . . .

It was only the odd exception—exceptions like Patrick Fourie—who resisted her charms.

As Lan stepped into a cotton dress she had picked out for the evening, she smiled to herself thinking about how she had never —*ever*—thought of her attractiveness in the form of 'charm' previously. What had brought on that particular idea?

The final feature of her body which she recognised was the small tattoo of a snow flower which she'd had done just above her hip; soon after she'd left her home behind. It'd been one of those adolescent, knee-jerk reactions to striking out on her own.

Actually, to tell the truth, she was somewhat ashamed of the tattoo now.

It wasn't even particularly delicately drawn.

Punctual to the point of madness, Lan was ready a full fifteen minutes before she had planned. It meant that she had the chance to look herself over in the full-length mirror, and to once again marvel at her long, black hair which flowed down to her waist.

Patrick Fourie hadn't been interested in her—*so what?*

She was certain that she would find someone at the picnic tonight . . . once she got on with this business about her parents; this *dreadfully* important information which Kyra was apparently just *dying* to tell her. Perhaps Lan didn't need to be alone.

Maybe she wasn't as much of a hopeless, solitary case as she'd always believed herself to be. The person she had *forced* herself to be ever since she had been snubbed by her parents.

Perhaps—someway; *somehow*—there was love out there for her.

And maybe even beneath the Celestial Stays Dome.

On arrival to the Crescent Gardens, Lan stepped out of the PEAR. She hovered on the landing pad, listening for the familiar mechanical *whine* as the visor cranked its way back down into the vehicle. Then she turned her attention out, to the Crescent Gardens.

The first thing she noticed was how a sharp, sweet scent of honey cut through the air. It immediately swept her back to a time in her childhood when they'd gone to visit their relatives in the countryside.

Although Lan couldn't have been older than about nine or ten, she recalled how her parents had treated their family members with barely concealed contempt; which was as they treated anyone who didn't build their lives around the ROCAF.

Lan recalled how one of her aunts—or had she been a *great* aunt?—had brought out an assortment of baked rolls. Each one of them had been smeared with a dollop of honey, harvested from the nearby hives. While she'd noticed her parents making scorned expressions to one another as they'd reluctantly partaken of their bread rolls and honey, Lan had been naïve enough just to enjoy the incredibly full, woody flavour.

When they'd left their family behind—to return to Shanghai—Lan couldn't understand her parents' bitter criticisms of their 'unsuccessful' country-bumpkin relatives.

She thought the way they lived—away from the smog, and the noise, and the towering skyscrapers—was just wonderful.

If she'd ever had the chance in her childhood, she would've traded all the asphalt, all the trappings of a modern city, for those green pastures; for the rolling hills; for the *fresh* air.

She recalled that one day she had actually fished through her parents' filing cabinets—where they kept all papers of importance —wanting to see confirmation that she was indeed their daughter; that there wasn't a Certificate of Adoption stashed away, hidden.

The Crescent Gardens were lit with what seemed like a myriad of tea lights; all of them a ghostly white colour. However, as Lan trod her way into the Gardens, between the ferns and the conifers, she realised that it was the plants themselves which glowed.

It was then that she recalled—because she hadn't been invited to *see*—the spectacle which Njhay Garcia—Louise William's lover, and the prominent scientific member of the Gardens—-had put on for Gofreddo Zito's father—*Costantino's*—visit.

She had heard from the members of the Security Division who'd been on duty that night about how the leaves themselves had glowed; that they'd needed no other illumination.

Lan could clearly remember wishing that she could've been there herself.

Well, she was here now.

As she trod her way along the path, the toe of one of the flat-soled shoes she'd chosen for the evening kicked a pine cone. She bent down and picked it up, examining it in the ethereal lighting coming off the plants. It was strange to see something which she associated so strongly with Earth, here . . . on the *Moon*. Then again, she supposed that those who worked in the garden—Louise and Njhay, among others—had swiftly grown used to this phenomenon.

For them, it was just as normal for them to go about their day's work in the garden as it was for Lan to go about her own day's work keeping the Celestial Stays Dome secure.

Lan emerged from a group of what she recognised as snow flowers—a sight common in China; and the original which had influenced the tattoo just above her hip. It was somewhat bizarre —but unarguably *beautiful*—to see all of the delicate white petals glimmering away. For a second, nostalgia caught her, and her heart thrummed up in her throat. For the shortest of moments she was certain she was going to cry. But, thankfully, someone called her away.

"You made it then?"

Lan looked up to see Louise staring back at her, a smile fixed on her lips. She had tousled her blond hair into a ragged ponytail and tied in several white and red rose petals.

Lan couldn't help but think that Louise looked a little like someone who'd just stepped off a hippie commune.

"Your hair is *gorgeous*," Louise said, reaching out to stroke Lan's hair, with a hypnotised look on her face.

Although Lan wasn't in the habit of letting people touch her hair, she allowed Louise to do so; only giving a slight flinch when her fingertips made contact.

Apparently satisfied, Louise drew back from Lan, still smiling, and asked, "So where is he? Where's your *hot* date?"

It was like someone had punched Lan directly in the solar plexus. And she nearly took a couple of steps back as if it'd been a physical blow. But she managed to keep her expression straight, to keep her wits about her. "I . . . I decided to come alone," she replied.

But Lan wasn't convinced that Louise even heard her, because, just like that, Louise's attention was snatched away by Alicia approaching.

Like Louise, Alicia had rose petals arranged in her hair, but —*unlike Louise*—Alicia only had white petals arranged in her brown hair. The two of them, side by side, looked like a pair of veritable Flower Children. But Lan held herself back from saying anything.

She barely knew either of them after all.

Thankfully, before Alicia got the chance to finish what Louise had begun, there was another distraction. When Lan looked, she saw that it was Mackenzie Angliss.

While Alicia and Louise had turned up to the picnic—if what looked to be a full-blown catered event with dozens of guests could be called a 'picnic'—as a pair of Flower Children, Mackenzie Angliss had shown up here in a severe, low-cut white top with a close-fitting trouser suit. If it hadn't been for the strappy sandals she wore, she might've looked more ready for the boardroom than for an impromptu picnic.

Lan allowed herself to relax slightly.

Skulking away nearby to Mackenzie, Lan recognised Miguel Cruz—the bookish guy who ran the Armstrong Archive. She would often see him in the gym, back at the Basements. From what she'd observed, she had to admit she was impressed. He wasn't one of those men who liked to pile as much weight onto the barbells as possible so that they could pump all their strength into a single rep; apparently in the hope that some 'babe' might be watching.

No, he was a proper lifter.

From what Lan had witnessed from a far, he had a strict routine based all around dozens of repetitions. Perhaps if she'd been more friendly-minded she would've asked him to spot for her on occasion; or she might've asked if she should spot for him.

The combination of the amount of people, and the relaxed atmosphere, eased her previous tensions about accepting the invitation to the picnic in the Crescent Gardens tonight.

In her worst imaginings, she had believed that it could turn out to be some nightmarish *couples'* outing . . . and with her there to be some kind of a third wheel.

Soon enough, it seemed that both Alicia and Louise's attention was firmly fixed onto Mackenzie Angliss, and, indeed, the two of them made their excuses before wandering off in her direction.

From a safe distance, Lan observed the swooping kisses being placed onto cheeks; the flappy, clappy *girl talk* going on. Lan had always believed the old observation that a group of strangers' laughter is by far the most forbidding sound in the entire universe.

And what she was witnessing right now was hardly much more welcoming. It was almost as if someone wished to hold up an example of what she would never have and thrust it in her face.

But—what could she say?—Lan had never been a people person . . . and she never would be.

"Uh, *hi.*"

Startled, Lan turned around.

Her heart fluttered up to her throat.

And her blood seemed to cease pouring through her veins.

Just for a moment.

It took her several seconds to consciously realise just who it was.

Just *who* was standing before her.

Patrick.

Patrick Fourie.

11

UNEXPECTED ENCOUNTER

*I*t *was a funny feeling*, not really knowing what to say when she set eyes on Patrick.

A whole flock of wonderings fluttered through her mind.

She couldn't manage to pin just one down.

Maybe it was his appearance.

Maybe it was the way he *looked*.

If anything, he looked *even more* ravishing than he had in the Shuttle Hangar.

The time when Lan had asked him here—*to the picnic*.

Tonight he wore a tuxedo, as all the men seemed to. She wondered out of which wardrobe he'd pulled it . . . and she wondered if she hadn't seen it on Gofreddo Zito in the past.

It did seem—*just a touch*—baggy on Patrick's prim frame.

She absorbed Patrick's strawberry-blond hair again.

Those hazel eyes.

And his bristling, tight muscles.

She knew all about *those* muscles.

The discipline required to build—and then *maintain*—them.

For the longest time, they just stood there, regarding one another.

Neither of them able to better Patrick's substandard, *Uh, hi* greeting.

Finally, Lan decided she should be the one to speak up.

"So," she said, "you *did* decide to come. You weren't so busy after all?"

Patrick blushed at this, and Lan actually felt a little bad. Because she realised that she didn't hold him culpable for saying 'no' to her back in the Hangar.

That was his prerogative.

She didn't want to make life awkward for *anyone*.

And, all the same, she hadn't come here to meet with Patrick.

She had come here to meet with Kyra.

To find out what she had to say about her parents.

Patrick's eyes skimmed over Lan's, and then shifted off to the crowd.

More and more people seemed to be streaming through the Crescent Gardens turnstiles.

All of them employees.

"I'm . . . *sorry*," Patrick began, turning back to Lan. "I'm sorry about turning you down in the Shuttle Hangar." Here he broke into a nervous grin. "You have no . . . ah . . . *idea* . . . no idea just how much of a surprise it was that, ah—"

Lan scrunched her eyebrows together. "That *what*?"

Although she didn't *feel* bitter, her words emerged from between her lips with more than a touch of bile. She supposed that was just her personality. She was naturally confrontational.

Patrick took a moment to draw breath—one of those profound respirations which went all the way down to the very pit of the stomach. He arched his shoulders back and then sighed it out, looking over the crowd as he did so.

Finally, he looked back at Lan. "I was surprised that a girl . . . a *woman*"—he caught himself—"like you would be interested in someone . . . someone like *me.*"

Lan was surprised by this statement.

Of course she wasn't an idiot . . . less than an hour or so ago she had been considering herself in her room; in the full length mirror; remarking at her own beauty.

She could tell that Patrick was caught up in her hair.

That he couldn't stop *staring* at it.

To tell the truth, she could hardly stop herself from staring at that chest of his.

She couldn't help wondering at just how tough it might be.

At how much force she might require to puncture his skin with her fingernails . . .

In a single movement, she snapped back onto Patrick's eyes, losing herself for several seconds. And then—a shift which came just as naturally to her as breathing or drinkin—she leaned into him.

Even as she felt his warmth, even as she consciously thought about how she would press her lips up against his, she thought about how wild this all was; about how *crazy* this must all seem. She almost expected Patrick to pull back. For him to evade her.

Like he had evaded her back in the Shuttle Hangar.

But, it seemed, he had had time to think.

He had had time to consider his mistakes.

And he had learned from them.

Lan reached around him quickly, seizing him in her hold. She watched the startled flinch of his eyelids as she surprised him with her strength. She liked to surprise . . . she *liked* people to underestimate her. It was her greatest weapon.

She gripped tightly to his shoulders, digging her fingertips into the tuxedo he wore. Feeling his skin beneath the fabric. How much force would it take? How much *force* would it take? It made her wonder . . .

She pressed her lips tightly to his.

Although he wasn't reluctant, he did hold himself back, as if he was afraid to give away too much all at once. It seemed ironic, in a way, that she who had always felt so apart from the rest of the world—*from other human beings*—found this act so natural now.

It felt as if *she* was the one on familiar ground.

Gently, though—*gradually*—Patrick eased his way into their kiss.

He tasted vaguely sweet; that same woodlike scent which clung to the air hung around him. He was clean, and well-muscled, and —*for tonight, at least*—all hers . . .

Lan lost track of time as they kissed; as their lips met together in an unbreakable rhythm, parting briefly before returning to one another all over again.

In the end, wanting to retain control, Lan made sure she was the one to break off the kiss. And when she did, she looked around; realised that quite a crowd was watching on.

Among the first rows of the crowd, she spotted Alicia and Louise, the two of them beside themselves, both clutching their hands up to their lips as if they were afraid of allowing their girlish giggles to sneak free of their mouths.

It was Louise who began to clap.

And Alicia who encouraged her.

Before she knew it, the whole assembled crowd was clapping her and Patrick, as if they'd just come through some life-and-death situation . . . or as if the two of them had somehow cropped up in the final scene of some overblown Hollywood film.

At least Patrick would know he wasn't the only one blushing this time.

12

THE CRESCENT GARDENS

*P*atrick *felt* as if his whole body was ready to melt. He felt the eyes all upon him. Nothing like this had ever happened to him; he never would've believed that anything like this *would* ever happen to him. But when he glanced down at his hand, and saw that he continued to entwine his fingers with Lan's, he realised that this was *real*.

Her touch was as good as any pinch to let him know this wasn't a dream.

When the crowd's applause had died down, and the two of them were together, Patrick realised how deeply he was flushing.

How much blood had surged to his cheeks.

He had always thought—having a naturally fair complexion— that he looked something like a tomato whenever he blushed. This realisation was made all the worse by his propensity to blush often. When he glanced up, Patrick realised that someone was approaching the two of them.

A girl . . . a *woman*.

She wore a beautifully patterned sari and had distinctive, tanned skin; silky smooth black hair. Although Patrick had never been on first-name terms with her, he knew her right away. It was Kyra Singh. Almost immediately he felt his chest tighten, and his stomach dip. A burning heat passed through his blood. This was the woman who had betrayed his best friend—the woman who had betrayed *Gofreddo* . . . and although Gofreddo might show nothing but kindness toward her—seeming as if he was the real-life incarnation of the old maxim 'turn the other cheek'—Patrick would have nothing to do with her.

If there was one thing which he had right down to his bones, it was a sense of loyalty.

He supposed he had picked up that particular quality from his father; although, while his father was only visibly loyal to the ranch—his family members were merely an *extension* of the ranch —Patrick's loyalty was for his friends.

And so it was on instinct that Patrick pushed the warming feeling out of his system, unlocked his fingers from Lan's, and straightened up in preparation for Kyra's approach.

When she was close enough for them to speak, Patrick made sure to make his tone of voice throaty; vaguely threatening. "I don't think you'll find any stories here," he said.

Kyra's eyes darted onto Patrick's, and he felt a sizzle right down to his gut.

Patrick knew that she was dangerous.

Everyone knew she was dangerous.

It was a wonder she hadn't been sent right back down Earth-side the second she'd been caught leaking the news story concerning Gofreddo's grandmother; and her burial at the Lunar One Monument, alongside her husband.

Kyra nodded to Lan. "I want to speak with her," she said.

Ready to break into a full-on tongue-lashing, to berate her for attempting to get some titbit concerning Gofreddo out of him, Patrick found himself taken off guard.

He was rendered speechless for several seconds.

And that was all it took for Lan to take a few steps away from him, and to give him an apologetic glance. As she trod off with Kyra, she mouthed something to him; something which Patrick interpreted as, *I'll explain later.*

When Lan had slipped out of sight, it was like Patrick had just come around from some delightful dream. Now that he didn't see her any longer—now that he no longer saw her sleek, black hair which reached her waist—it was as if her spell was broken.

As if his capacity for rational thought had returned.

Just what the *hell* had he been thinking?

. . . And with all these people watching on.

If Kyra and Lan were truly friends then he knew that he could never allow his attraction toward Lan to develop any further than the passionate kiss they had shared moments ago. Granted, Lan was gorgeous, and she would surely give him many fitful, sleepless nights over the course of the next week as he churned his memories of their kiss, but that was all it could be.

Because he valued his friendship with Gofreddo above all else.

When Patrick had turned his attention fully away from the last spot he had spied Lan—between a pair of bushes he couldn't think to name—he finally settled on Gofreddo, Alicia, Louise and Njhay, all standing close by; each of them munching on whatever canapé Alicia had seen fit to prepare for the night's event.

With a final look back to where he had last seen Lan—and wondering whether she might return to him, apologising for the *faux pas* of being seen with Kyra—Patrick finally ventured over to the pair of couples, decided that he would stick around for as long as was polite before leaving them to enjoy the remainder of their evening.

He needed to learn to trust his gut more.

It *had* been a mistake to come to the picnic tonight.

13

PREVIOUS EVENT SEQUENCE

lthough it'd been extremely hard to do, Lan had broken away from Patrick. Her thoughts had rapidly spun out of control; so much so that she had largely failed to notice the large crowd which'd gathered around them. And then *applauded*.

She had needed to get away—*away* from the intensity of the moment.

Kyra's appearance had been a surreptitious excuse to do just that.

The two of them walked the shingle pathway, between the flowering tulips; all of them glowing faintly from whatever chemical cocktail Njhay had cooked up. They were an assortment of light colours; of peaches, of sapphires, and of creams.

Sometimes Lan wished for her childhood all over again; for the chance to lose herself in some area of study . . . an area of study completely *unrelated* to the ROCAF, or to aeroplanes.

She could've been someone important; perhaps even a botanist like Njhay Garcia, or whatever his official title happened to be.

Might she have a very different perspective on the Celestial Stays Dome—*on the world*—if she had qualified for something else?

If she'd given something more substantial than 'security' a go?

It was with a slight smile that Lan thought of how much she secretly enjoyed the steady weight of a blaster pistol stashed into a thigh holster. And she loved the buzz of adrenalin which accompanied a chase through a busy area . . . bumping into people; demanding they get out of the way while she tracked the perpetrator.

She wondered if she should've become a cop.

That would've at least been *similar* to what her parents had wanted.

She would've gone to work every day in a uniform.

Once more, she scolded herself for thinking about her parents at all; for caring *at all* about what they thought of her. And then, realising that they'd managed to get to her inside and out—because wasn't she accompanying Kyra here so that she might hear what she had to tell her about her parents?—Lan came to a sudden halt, then reached out and grabbed Kyra a little briskly by her elbow.

Kyra halted her advance instantly; Lan assumed that there were very few people beneath the Celestial Stays Dome who could truly resist her physical strength.

Perhaps Gofreddo Zito.

Maybe Patrick Fourie . . . she would have to see about *that*.

"There's not much time," Kyra said, her tone hurried either by the sense of the situation or Lan's tight hold on her arm.

"No," Lan replied, matter-of-factly. "Tell me what you have to say *now*."

Kyra let out a sigh, but it was more out of exasperation than impatience. As if she realised that she was in danger somehow. Could it be that she was intimidated by her?

It took Lan about a split second to realise that she couldn't care less . . . in fact, most likely, it would work in her favour.

Kyra held herself still, apparently considering whether or not she should say whatever it was she needed to say here; or if she should just call the whole thing off.

If Kyra did choose to call the whole thing off then Lan could draw a line under the episode; conclude that Kyra was full of shit after all, that she had been playing games with Lan; perhaps trying to get herself on the inside track with a member of the Security Division.

For a journalist like Kyra that would surely be a mighty bonus . . .

"Are you unhooked?" Kyra asked.

Lan gave her a stern nod.

She had switched off the Link as soon as Kyra had approached.

She had kind of assumed that it would be a necessary step when interacting on any level with her.

Kyra pressed her lips tightly together, and then surveyed their surroundings, as if she was unconvinced that they were alone. Finally, she turned back into Lan, apparently satisfied. "I was filing a report," she began. "A *story*."

Lan had assumed that since Kyra's outing as an undercover journalist—ever since her relaying of stories to some media outlet—she had been cut off from all contact with the Earth. She had assumed it would be the *bare minimum* that the Celestial Stays administration would arrange after her highly public—and highly *embarrassing*—leaks of Gofreddo Zito's grandmother's burial.

Kyra gave a light smile, the first sign that she was at all comfortable with the meeting which was currently taking place. "I know what you're thinking." She held up her hands. "And don't worry—it's all above board . . . well, it's all *above board* with Celestial Stays; if that's what you're worried about." Here her smile developed into a *wicked* grin. "Frau Köhler is a most *calculating* woman; she knows how to take any situation, turn it on its head, and make it work to her advantage."

Frau Köhler—*Karolin Köhler*—was of course the owner of Celestial Stays. And she wasn't one of those hands-off CEOs. She liked to be down on the ground—or up on the *Moon*, as the case often was—getting her hands dirty with the details.

Kyra continued, "She decided that rather than being a threat, I might well be an *asset*." She shrugged her shoulders as if it was clear as day what the arrangement was, and that she was only spelling all this out in the interests of clarity; of establishing the *facts*. "She decided to keep who I am under wraps—*Earthside*—claiming that nobody knows who the source of the leaks was . . . that way I can continue to leak information to Earth, though, this time, it'll be with Frau Köhler's blessing."

Lan saw an opportunity to break in. "You mean that you're working some sort of clandestine publicity for Celestial Stays?"

Kyra broke into a grin. "You could call it that." Her grin slackened a touch about the corners, and her gaze slipped away.

Lan allowed their conversation to slip away into silence, and then she decided to shift its focus back onto the matter at hand. "So," Lan said, "if you've got your back all covered—courtesy of Frau Köhler—then why all the secrecy?"

Kyra's eyes darted about now, as if she was picking at the shadows, turning each one over in her mind, trying to work out if there might be some movement. "Well, you know the protocol," she said. "You know the *procedure* with Earthside Comms."

Indeed, just like every other employee beneath the Celestial Stays Dome—but perhaps more than most after her time spent behind a desk at Security HQ—Lan knew that any communication with Earth was strictly monitored; that it passed through a series of filters before arriving to an employee's Link. As far as Lan understood it, it had to do with morale.

There was no beating around the bush, getting someone to the Moon was an expensive undertaking. And one which Frau Köhler —a shrewd businesswoman; as Kyra had already alluded to —acknowledged.

The whole issue revolved around family crises. It was no secret that often those who chose to come and work for Celestial Stays didn't have the most stable of households back home on Earth; and an unstable household, as Lan knew first-hand, would often produce issues to be attended to.

Issues which might distract employees from their duties.

And so, seeing that a rotation lasted *only* eighteen months, it was a condition of each and every one of their contracts that they agreed to have their contact with Earth limited.

In Lan's case this really hadn't been a big deal.

In fact, she could consciously recall skimming through her contract—she never *truly* read *all* the small print—and her eye catching that particular clause. She'd even felt a wry smile sneak onto her lips at its appearance there, assuring herself—as if she needed assuring—that this particular clause wouldn't cause her any difficulty whatsoever.

If she had any Earthside Comms throughout her rotation, there was little doubt that they would be bland job offers; or dull, form-letters from co-workers asking her to give them a personal reference for whatever post they happened to be applying for.

Now, though, now that Kyra seemed on edge—that she had some potentially *explosive* information surrounding Lan's parents —Lan wondered if she hadn't been somewhat wreckless in her attitude to that particular clause of her contract with Celestial Stays.

Because . . . well, if something had happened . . . if something had gone wrong . . . she *would* want to know . . . wouldn't she?

It sent a strange, shimmering heat through her blood to think that one of her colleagues might've been filtering her personal communications while sat at the desk beside her.

Kyra's eyes found Lan's once more. "Well, it was just . . . you know, a casual thing . . . I've been working closely with Frau Köhler, the two of us working out some particularly positive stories to send down to Earth. It was while I was sending the information across; *phoning it in,* you might say"—here she smiled slightly, but the smile didn't last—"that I thought to check over the current news headlines."

Lan's heart dropped.

Her muscles stiffened.

Kyra's expression was grave now; none of the light-hearted nature which'd accompanied their walk through the Crescent Gardens was present.

Lan prepared herself for the worst.

Kyra continued, "I've always had a good head for remembering names—*faces* . . . I don't know why, but it's something which has always just *stuck* with me . . ." She glanced off over the glowing garden; in the direction of murmuring voices of the others. "It was when I was poring over the headlines; looking for anything which might affect Celestial Stays—that's another one of my agreements with Frau Köhler; to search out negative stories about the company and either stop them dead or mitigate their effects. But it was more than just the Celestial Stays in the headline. When I turned my attention to scanning the article itself I came across a pair of familiar names, uh . . ." Here she trailed away, as if she couldn't continue. But she forced herself onwards. "Yŏng *Niu* and Jié *Niu*." She held her breath, and then stared Lan in the eye.

The names were, of course, those of Lan's parents.

Lan waited a long moment, feeling herself caught up in the suspense.

She wanted to know . . . she wanted to know *now* . . . and yet, at the same time, she didn't want to know at all; it was almost as if she might be able to change the reality simply by holding her hands over her ears and humming. As if she was still a child.

"Well," Kyra continued, eyeing Lan, as if she was double-guessing herself as to whether or not she should continue. The way Kyra was going on, Lan was ready to strangle the information out of her if she had to. "It was so *weird*; how they went into the details about how their daughter had signed up to go into space—that she had signed on to work for Celestial Stays; and, during the journey she had sadly passed away from the stress . . ."

Kyra stopped short, glancing up.

Lan's throat felt swollen, and she could feel a heaviness at the corners of her eyes. Her whole body was rigid with tension. She couldn't understand—*couldn't understand at all*.

"I looked into the details; there've been no reported deaths on any of the trips from Earth to the Dome . . . I judged the article as being so serious that I even went to Frau Köhler; asked her what we should do about it."

"And?" Lan replied, hearing the tears in her voice now.

"She was measured, like she always is. She looked over my fact-checking, confirmed what we already knew to be true; that no one has died during that journey."

"What does it mean?" Lan asked, although she of course already knew the answer.

Kyra said nothing.

The silence grew between the two of them once again.

And then it dawned on Lan. "That's the reason for secrecy," Lan said, "Frau Köhler didn't want me to know anything about this— that my own parents faked my death?"

Kyra remained very still.

Then she gave a stern nod.

Lan felt a mixture of emotions; gratitude that Kyra had risked her own neck—*taken liberties with what was surely her last chance*—so that Lan might know the truth. But there was mostly just numbness . . . to know that all Lan's worst fears; that her parents couldn't have cared less about her; had proven true.

And *then* some . . .

Lan forced herself to stay in the moment.

To *not* break down in a tearful heap.

"Was there anything else?" she asked, her voice shaking.

Kyra's lips parted for a fraction of a second, and then she caught herself; gave a shake of her head. "No," she said. "That was everything." She glanced off across the surrounding foliage, though this time it was out of awkwardness, rather than paranoia.

Acting on impulse—*one of those impulses her parents had tried, and failed, to squeeze out of her*—Lan launched herself forward, and embraced Kyra. She squeezed her tightly to her chest, using the same force she had used to spin Kyra around; to get her to stop her advance and tell her directly what was going on. "Thank you," Lan just about got out, through her half-closed lips. "Thank you for telling me this."

CLEANSING ALL SYSTEMS

*L*an *kicked herself* off from the side of the swimming pool. She felt her body glide through the water; her arms gently sweeping out and around her as she prepared to launch into the rhythm of the front crawl.

Her abdomen ached from the thousand-or-so sit-ups she had forced herself through back up in the gym. Her upper arms felt as if they might drop off at any moment from the elaborate workout.

But she had to keep going.

She had to keep ploughing through the water.

Everything was more simple when she was in the water, when she could peer through her goggles at the inky-blue, rectangular lines at the base of the pool; the ones which guided her.

When she reached the other end, she performed a neat tumble-roll, and then resumed her progress. She counted off the lengths as she went. She'd reached forty-three now, and she had no intention of stopping until she got to fifty.

Or maybe she'd keep going to sixty?

Seventy?

Eighty?

Ninety?

. . . One hundred?

Where would it stop?

As Lan tumbled through into her forty-fourth length, she felt a sharp pain in her left side. It was sharp enough to make her wince. And to send a jangling sensation through her arm.

She came to a halt.

Stood up in the pool.

Her shoulders just breaking the surface.

She was used to pain, of course, and she had a variety of strategies to manage it.

The foremost of those was to take gulping lungfuls of air.

Or, in other words, to simply take a *timeout*.

She steadied herself, only realising now that her vision had gone all blurry about the edges; that the carved, sharp lines of the archways and pillars surrounding the pool had become curved.

Her heart beat loudly in her eardrums.

But she had succeeded at her task.

She now thought of nothing—*nothing at all . . .*

Only the pain.

Pain and *exertion*.

"Howdy."

The word was almost like a knife to Lan's gut.

She pivoted around, restricted by the water's resistance.

There, standing on the side of the pool, wearing a swimming suit and with her hair neatly tucked away beneath a rubbery, black skullcap—*very much like the one which Lan herself wore*—was Alicia. Alicia Brennan.

The last thing Lan was in the mood for was company.

With a vague, borderline polite, "Hey," Lan eased her aching body through the water and over to the steps which led out of the pool.

Attempting not to show any sign of the extreme pain currently wracking her body, Lan favoured her right arm, putting all her weight onto it. She was glad that she hadn't damaged her shooting hand. That really *would* have been a tragedy.

When she bent over herself to pick up the tightly wrapped towel she'd left on the tiles alongside the swimming pool, Lan felt a fresh wave of pain. She winced, but kept her face turned away from Alicia so that she wouldn't see. She didn't like *anybody* to see any sort of weakness in her.

"Don't let me stop you," Alicia said, a smile in her voice.

Pushing the pain down, Lan turned her head casually in Alicia's direction. "Oh, you're not," she said, only telling half a lie; it wasn't like she'd be able to get in many more lengths after she'd pulled that muscle in her side. And then, deciding that she needed to be a bit friendlier, Lan attempted to lighten her tone of voice, saying, "Enjoy your swim."

As Lan trudged her way to the changing-room entrance—doing her best not to show off her limp—she felt Alicia's eyes burning into her back. When Lan had reached the doorway, she thought she'd made it. That she'd managed to break free from Alicia's company.

But, right at the last moment, Alicia called her back.

"Hey, Lan?"

Her back to Alicia, Lan squeezed her eyes shut out of apprehension at the coming exchange.

Why wouldn't people just leave her alone?

Why was it that people were always *trying* to make her join in?

Why didn't *people* get it into their thick skulls that some human beings were just *designed* to be alone?

Human beings like her . . .

Sensing that there would be more trouble ahead if she didn't interact with Alicia right at that moment, Lan turned around. She stared back into Alicia's smiling features, and attempted to raise a smile of her own. "That was quite some show," Alicia said. "You know, the other day, in the Crescent Gardens—at the picnic." As if it was necessary, and with a wider smile still, she added, "That kiss between you and Patrick?"

Already, Lan could sense the unease creeping into Alicia's voice. There was something intrinsic to Lan's personality which made people *feel* uneasy in her presence. Something which *rubbed them up the wrong way*. In truth, Lan hadn't thought about the kiss all that much; she had been more preoccupied with the grander issue of her parents . . . and just precisely what'd led to them claiming that their only daughter—their only *child*—had died out in space.

But she wasn't about to open up that box of tricks all over again.

The brutal exercising afterward might cost her a leg this time . .
.

Lan met Alicia's eye, trying to divine what it was she wanted. She feigned what she hoped would appear to be a *more authentic* smile, and then said, "Yeah."

In the forefront of her mind, Lan hoped that this dampened response would suffice; that Alicia would catch the hint that Lan had no interest in interfacing with her.

But Alicia, it seemed, wouldn't be shaken off so easily.

"You should see Patrick," Alicia said, reaching to tuck a stray lock of hair up into her rubber skullcap. "Whenever we bring you up—whenever we *mention* That Kiss—he goes all red." She raised half of her mouth in a wry smile. "Really, it's unbecoming of a red-blooded, harum-scarum Shuttle pilot."

Lan truly had nothing to say to this. "That's . . . unfortunate."

Alicia smiled wider. "*I'll* say," she replied, and then, after a quick glance to the pool, and apparently deciding that she wasn't going in *just yet*, she took a few steps toward Lan. When she spoke again, her smile was less pronounced; and her voice was decidedly more sombre. "There was one thing I needed to talk to you about."

Deciding that active disengagement didn't seem to be working, Lan decided to shift her tactics.

She needed to be more direct.

She turned away from Alicia, headed into the changing rooms. "I'm on shift in twenty minutes."

This was truthful; though, what Alicia didn't know was that Lan could be all dried off and dressed within *five* minutes. She'd still make it to Security HQ with plenty of time to spare.

"It won't take a second," Alicia said.

When Lan thought back on the meeting, she decided that it had been Alicia's tone of voice which'd prevented her simply plodding off into the changing rooms. She was so used to Alicia's happy-go-lucky tone that to hear any other sort of voice seemed out of place.

Odd.

Lan stood her ground, reluctantly curious now. "Okay," she said.

Alicia gave her a rugged smile. "It's about Kyra."

" 'Kyra' ?" Lan replied, furrowing her brow.

Alicia nodded in reply. "Now, look, far be it from me to tell you who should be your friends around here, but it's just . . . well, you know what she was implicated in . . . *everyone* knows the gossip;

and I can tell you, from a position of confidence, that what they say about the gossip is pretty much right on."

Lan still wasn't sure how to take this.

She felt her brain squeezing in on itself.

What *was* this?

Alicia continued, "I don't know how you truly feel about Patrick—but if what I observed of that kiss is anything to go by, you feel *a lot*. You need to know how highly he values his friendship with Gofreddo. How *protective* he is of Gofreddo."

" 'Protective' ?" Lan replied, now intrigued. "How do you mean?"

Alicia gave a slight frown, as if she was struggling to explain the matter to herself. "You have to understand that Gofreddo has always had trust issues. When you grow up the son of Costantino Zito everybody wants a piece of you."

Lan thought she could feel her heart bleeding for him.

Alicia continued, "He takes a long time in weeding out people—in working out just *who* he can trust." She gave a shake of her head. "He has to take care . . . as you saw only recently he got himself into trouble . . . with letting his defences down."

Despite the fact that Gofreddo clearly had uncountable billions to weep into, Lan could at the very least empathise on a human level. Especially after her parents had declared in the media that she—*herself*—had been killed out in space . . .

Lan decided to short circuit the conversation. "So," she put in, "what you're saying is that you don't want me seeing Kyra anymore; that if I have any designs on Patrick then I'll have to break off contact with her . . . otherwise *I* might be another leak?"

Alicia was rendered stunned for several long seconds, as if she was attempting to explain in another way. But, already, Lan could see that she had summarised things quite succinctly.

Lan arched an eyebrow. "Just a bit paranoid, don't you think?"

Alicia eased into her more typical, friendly smile and tone of voice. "You might think that, but I've been close by when these things have happened . . . it wasn't pleasant . . . not when it was the one I love . . ."

Alicia blushed slightly, as if she'd become a little too candid for her comfort.

Lan was glad to see that Alicia could be just as easily embarrassed as herself.

It humanised her.

Alicia jerked her thumb over her shoulder, indicating the still water of the pool over her shoulder. "Well," she said, "guess it's time for me to get in or go home, huh?"

Despite herself, Lan couldn't do anything but return the smile. "Suppose so," she said. "See you around."

"All righty," Alicia replied, then made off for the pool steps.

Lan lingered a moment in the doorway to the changing rooms.

The reason why escaped her.

When she thought about it later, she wondered if—on some level—she had been *enjoying* Alicia's company. And then she decided that it could hardly be any other case.

Because what was wrong with basking in human warmth?

15

SHUTTLE HANGAR

*P*atrick *eased himself* along on the creeper. He squinted as he attempted to make out the intricate wiring within the panel he was currently inspecting. The torch he held in his hand shod a slightly mangy glow into the hole. It mangled colours to some extent which made it more difficult to make out the wires with any degree of certainty. Just as he was considering flipping onto a head-up display function through the Link—one which would dot his vision and show him, with no-nonsense clarity, which were the parts he sought—he heard footsteps on the Shuttle Hangar's cement floor. He paused briefly before sliding himself back out, imagining—*from one of the more imaginative regions of his mind*—that it might be Lan Niu coming by to pay him a visit . . . and that she'd have her hair all combed down, hanging at her waist . . . and that she might be wearing a fur coat . . . with nothing on underneath.

When Patrick emerged into the harsh light of the Shuttle

Hangar, however, he soon saw that his wildest dreams had failed to come true. It was—*more predictably*—Gofreddo.

Just as Patrick did, Gofreddo wore the grimy-grey flight overalls which were distinctive to those who'd either recently arrived to the Dome or who were soon to depart. Or those, like Patrick and Gofreddo, whose duty it was to come and go from the Dome; day after day.

"Whatcha doing down there on the floor?" Gofreddo asked, smiling widely.

Patrick dipped into his overalls and removed a greasy rag. He used the rag to wipe off his hands, although he'd hardly so much as touched the Shuttle. "Oh, just taking a look," Patrick replied.

Gofreddo took a few steps up to the Shuttle. He rapped his fist against its bodywork, causing it to give an even, dull *clunk-clunk* which echoed momentarily about the Shuttle Hangar. "This piece of junk should do fine," he said, turning to look out through the Hangar doors; and across the lunar plains. "It's not like we've been abusing it recently."

Patrick cast his mind back to the many aerobatics they'd performed only the day before. The two of them taking turns— with grinning expressions—to try and scare the other out of his wits.

It'd been after that particular session that Patrick had noticed something amiss with the Shuttle's thrusters . . . and if he hadn't gone to the trouble of giving the Shuttle a solid once-over it was likely they'd have found themselves stranded out on the plains one of these days.

And—with Celestial Stays clientele aboard—that certainly would've been an issue.

Although he was his best friend, sometimes Patrick couldn't help but curse Gofreddo for his carefree ways. It was *fine* for Gofreddo Zito to have a devil-may-care attitude—he always had his rich daddy to fall back on . . . all that Patrick had to fall back on was his father's ranch; and he already knew, for a fact, that he wasn't welcome there.

Not unless he was returning for good.

If Gofreddo kept up with these habits of his—these seemingly insignificant *oversights* when it came to Shuttle maintenance—Patrick had little doubt that there would be some kind of accident just around the corner. And so, it was with this on his mind that he rose up off the creeper, straightened his back, and squared his shoulders. He needed to be direct. *Unambiguous.*

Anything else would be dishonesty.

"Fred?" Patrick said.

Gofreddo continued to peer out across the lunar plains. "Hmm?" he replied, his mind clearly other places.

"It's just . . . ah, these last few days . . . when I've been doing maintenance on the Shuttles—you know, *routine* stuff . . ."

Gofreddo turned around now, and Patrick noticed that his complexion was somewhat washed out; that his eyes appeared sunken in their sockets.

Patrick hated to pry into Gofreddo's personal life—mainly because it was clearly a no-go zone for anyone who wasn't either Gofreddo's family or his lover; Alicia—but he could tell from Gofreddo's expression that he had something on his mind.

Perhaps this was the wrong time.

As if taking up the mantle from Patrick, Gofreddo put in, "Do you ever look about this place—about the Dome—and think that this is all so much . . . uh . . ." he apparently searched for the word in English ". . . *small fry?*"

" 'Small fry' ?" Patrick replied, realising that he'd been thrown

93

off course, but deciding that he should pick another moment to bring up his concerns with Gofreddo. "In what way?"

Gofreddo fed Patrick a sneaking smile. "You know what I have always wanted? Do you know what I have *truly* always wanted?"

Patrick thought back to Gofreddo's much-publicised life down on Earth. As a neutral observer—as he had been before they'd met up here, beneath the Celestial Stays Dome—Patrick would've assumed that Gofreddo lived his life with one goal, and one goal only, fixed firmly in his mind:

Hedonism.

A complete dedication to pleasure and all its trimmings.

Now, though, he knew Gofreddo better.

Knew that there were murky, bottomless depths to his personality.

And impossible heights to his aspiration.

"What have you always wanted?" Patrick asked.

"I did not know until I learned of my grandfather—until I learned that he was a great explorer; one of those buried at the Lunar One Monument." He paused here for a long moment, and Patrick wondered if something had stuck in his throat. But he continued suddenly, as if he hadn't stopped at all. "It has been in my blood, all my life, but it is not until now that I have had the opportunity to *know* my destiny; to *embrace* it."

Patrick felt his mind swilling in and out.

His body was somewhat stiff . . . as if he might be on the brink of breaking.

All things considered, he'd spent a long while down on the creeper these past few days. He wondered if that constantly curved and curled posture was to blame.

Although Patrick had had the inkling that, as Gofreddo said, he carried a great deal of lofty aspirations about with him, it had never been put into words as he was doing at this very moment.

"What's your destiny?" Patrick asked.

Gofreddo pursed his lips, and set his hand on his hip. Then he stared Patrick back directly in his eye. "If I tell you," he said. "If I *confide* in you, then you must promise me that you shall never share it with another soul."

The intense, stern expression on Gofreddo's face was almost too much for Patrick to take. He had the urge to crack up in laughter . . . and yet, at the same time, he knew that that would be the very worst response he could make right now.

Patrick met Gofreddo's eye. "I promise," he said.

Lips slightly parted, Gofreddo made something between a *grunt* and a *groan* at the back of his throat. "I wish also to explore—to tread in my grandfather's footsteps. I want to *explore* the universe."

Patrick was on the brink of asking him just *how* he was going to achieve this, before he reminded himself—*silently*—that this was Gofreddo Zito he was dealing with; heir to one of the most substantial fortunes on Earth.

Because he felt that he had to say something, Patrick asked, "You mean like a spaceship? You're planning on exploring the universe in a *spaceship?*"

Gofreddo smiled warmly. "That is exactly what I plan." Gofreddo's expression shifted away from its easy smile; the outline of a frown appearing on his lips. "Would you be interested in joining my voyage?"

"What?" Patrick said, unable to conceal his surprise.

Although the situation felt like it demanded that Gofreddo's smile should return, he remained with the same stern-faced expression. "I would like my friends and family around me, on this voyage, the ones who mean the most to me . . . the ones who I can most *trust*."

Patrick allowed himself a moment to reflect on what Gofreddo was saying; just the *grandness* of the scale. He knew what it meant, of course. Although Patrick might know next to nothing about space exploration, one of the few things he did know was that it was often a one-way trip. And from what Gofreddo said—if he was serious about pushing back frontiers—then this would almost certainly be a one-way trip.

Patrick opened his mouth to reply, but Gofreddo hushed him with the subtlest of gestures; a raised palm.

"Do not give me your answer today," he said, and then—*and only then*—transitioned into his familiar, easy smile. "But do give it to me soon . . . when you have had time to think about it . . ."

There was a long pause—a slip into silence—and Patrick was certain that Gofreddo had lost his train of thought.

But then, finally, he said, "Tell no one."

16

SPEED VERSUS TIME

*a*s Lan moved, she felt the tightness down her left side from the injury she'd given herself in the pool . . . or the one she had *exacerbated* in the pool. She felt the steady, familiar weight of her blaster pistol strapped to her thigh as she left the PEAR behind, arriving on the landing strip before the Lunar Grand. Her brain felt as worn and weary as her body.

She had had what seemed like an age to think about the revelations—about the news which Kyra had revealed to her. As it turned out, it didn't matter how much she exercised, she could never quite manage to get her mind fully off the facts . . . that her parents had effectively killed her off.

If only in their own minds.

She had more questions, of course, notably among them just *why* they had gone to the trouble of contacting the media to do so; and then there was the creepier thought which troubled her, that they had known she had taken up a contract with Celestial Stays.

They *knew* she was working on the Moon.

How much else did they know about her?

How much else had they been able to fathom?

She had to admit that, throughout the past few days, she had been somewhat cautious in how she'd moved about the Celestial Stays Dome. It was her belief—indeed the only working explanation she had—that her parents had some sort of a private investigator keeping watch on her. How else did they know what she was up to?

Her assignment today was to escort a family from the hotel to the Shuttle Hangar, and then off along on their excursion. It seemed that Lan's boss—*Duval*—had taken note of her previous, successful outing. Well, she hadn't *shot* anyone, at least . . . and, if she pushed her imagination just a little, she could make herself believe that she had *saved* that small boy who'd wandered about from any untoward damage. She could draw on that memory of the family thanking her.

As she waited in the Lunar Grand lobby, she turned her mind back to *that* kiss; the one she'd shared with Patrick Fourie. It seemed almost like it'd happened years ago, as if it was some memory of her lost youth. That whole evening had been unreal; from beginning to end.

She recalled when she'd returned to the picnic, following her meeting with Kyra, and had noticed that Patrick had already gone off home. After the chat with Alicia, she at least had an inkling of why that was; that Patrick believed Lan was somehow *in league* with Kyra . . . the one who had betrayed the Mighty, All-Powerful Gofreddo Zito.

The Link informed Lan—through her inner earpiece—that the guests were drawing close. As she always did, she had set a proximity alert for the guests she'd been made responsible for that day. It aided her to stay sharp; to not allow her brain to drift. If she'd learned one thing from working security all her life, it was that you needed to keep your thoughts fully fixed on the task at hand.

Because it might cost more than your own life.

It might cost the life of your client.

Prompted by the slight *hum* from her earpiece, she shifted her attention to the lift at the end of the lobby. She watched on as the bronze doors swept out of view to reveal the lift's occupants.

One of the first skills which Lan had really worked on when she'd first started working security was her ability at observation. It was an underestimated, subtle skill. But one which had saved her more times than she could count.

In an instant, she absorbed the group of people.

A mother.

A father.

And a son—thirteen, fourteen years old?

The mother and father were sharply dressed in their burgundy overalls—the ones which were provided by Celestial Stays for the guests. Although these were standard-issue clothing, Lan couldn't help but notice the couple's straight-backed poise; how the two of them tilted their heads back ever so slightly, pointing their chin just out ahead.

It was a gesture—a *pose*—which Lan was more than familiar with.

It was the same pose her parents would strike.

Immediately, she pinned the mother and father as belonging to some disciplined element of the armed forces. Which one exactly, she would have to guess. But, judging from their appearance, their fair complexions, and their Anglo-Saxon features, she supposed them to be either European or North American. Lan shifted her attention to the son.

Saw how he hung back off his parents' heels.

Instantly, she noticed his slack shoulders; the way he walked with his forehead facing the floor, as if there was something incessantly interesting about the ersatz marble beneath his feet.

She recognised this, too, of course.

In another context—*at another time*—that boy could quite easily have been herself.

How many times had she struck that pose as a young girl, feeling ridiculous to be tagging along in her parents' jet stream?

Lan put her observations to one side in her conscious mind, now knowing how she should approach this situation; how she should tailor her manner to these particular members of the Celestial Stays clientele. She stepped up to the family, pressed on a smile. "Good morning," she said. "I trust you slept well."

Apparently positively noting her deliberately direct, no-nonsense tone, the father reached out his hand for her to shake. "Good morning," he said, taking her hand. "General Michaels, and family."

The handshake was over just as soon as it began, but she continued to feel the father's strong, unflinching grip for another few seconds after. She judged the father's accent to be Midwestern American. She had always been good at placing accents.

That'd been another skill she'd picked up when she'd learned observation.

She turned her attention onto the mother and the son, giving each of them a firm nod by way of greeting. She could tell from the way that this family was structured that the father was the dominating force. That he was the *representative* of the entire family.

By shaking his hand, Lan had, in effect, shaken them all by the hand.

As she led them toward the landing strip located outside the Lunar Grand, she caught the son's eye. He met her gaze for only a moment, but she detected that constant feeling of fear peering out at her from just beneath the surface.

It was almost like travelling back in time.

If she could say something to herself, back when she'd been a child, then what would it be?

She couldn't say for sure ...

The PEAR brought them to the Shuttle Hangar where they were immediately greeted by Gofreddo Zito. The whole family, of course, recognised Gofreddo; it seemed that, as had been the case throughout Gofreddo's life, his whole existence had been broadcast through a constant stream of tabloid headlines and *scandalous* images. His current situation, working as an everyman Shuttle pilot, hadn't escaped the attention of the world at large.

The family, though, adhering to their apparently strict sense of military discipline, made no comment in Gofreddo's direction, beyond the father greeting him with a handshake; the way he apparently treated all strangers.

Lan was conscious of her heart beating hard against her ribcage as she walked through the Shuttle Hangar. Although she had tried to rid herself of such *frivolous* thoughts over the past few days, she couldn't help but realise that this was Patrick Fourie's workplace; and that she might bump into him at any given moment.

What would she do?

What would she *say*?

Those reprimands—or whatever Alicia's 'chat' had construed—continued to ring in her ears; and they made her feel overly cautious about saying or doing anything that might be out of place.

It was here that she caught herself, wondering why it was that she cared so much. But—before she could draw the obvious conclusion—she was distracted by Gofreddo.

"We're gonna be taking you out to the North Pole, swinging you back to the Apollo 11 landing site, before finishing up at the Lunar One Monument—if that sounds all right by you?"

Lan studied Gofreddo's face, noting the dark circles beneath his eyes. The way that his eyeballs seemed almost to sink back in their sockets. His mouth barely squeezed open to allow his words out through the gap, and when he did speak, his words were more like an elongated *grumble* than a sentence.

"That sounds just fine," the father replied, again speaking for the entire family.

"All righty, then," Gofreddo put in, jerking his thumb in the direction of the steps leading up into the Shuttle. "Climb on aboard."

Lan couldn't help but notice that tiniest of details in Gofreddo's speech; that 'All righty' which she'd come to consider something of a trademark whenever Alicia Brennan spoke.

She supposed that was what happened when a pair of people got together; they began to learn one another's habits; one another's quips and tics.

What did that say about her?

Did it make her a purer, more individual person to have lived her life in solitude?

. . . Or did it just make her *lonely*?

Once they'd got themselves all boarded onto the Shuttle, they set off on the expedition.

Throughout the trip, Lan studied Gofreddo closely, watching him observing the father—or the *General*, as she'd heard his son referring to him the few times he'd had the nerve to raise his voice.

At the beginning of the Shuttle trip, Gofreddo had taken it easy on his passengers; he had gone through with a standard, steady take-off before taking a leisurely glide over the lunar plains which surrounded the Celestial Stays Dome. But then Lan had very clearly seen the sidelong glance which Gofreddo had slipped the General—the subtlest sliver of a smile the General had given him in return. And Gofreddo had entered his element.

With everyone strapped in tightly, he had led them through a sequence of aerobatics, turning them upside down with loop-the-loops; twisting them into a corkscrew with barrel-rolls; before finishing them off with a series of high-pitch assents followed by stomach-crunching dips back toward the lunar surface. By the time they were through with the tour—after they'd visited all the sights which Gofreddo had had in mind—the General was beaming from ear to ear. When Lan cast a glance back over her shoulder, to the mother and the son, she saw that they'd turned quite a pale colour. The son, in particular, looked as if he was in danger of losing his last meal.

They pulled back into the Shuttle Hangar and Gofreddo parked them up, rolling the tension from his shoulders before getting up to his feet and casting a satisfied look over his passengers.

Apparently realising that neither Lan, the mother or the son had had a particularly great time during the trip, he turned the entirety of his attention onto the General, who was already up and out of his seat himself and pumping Gofreddo's hand in appreciation.

Once they'd got back off the Shuttle, Lan felt a sense of disappointment.

Disappointment that she hadn't bumped into Patrick.

That he didn't appear to be on duty right now.

Whatever it was that had passed between them at the picnic a few nights ago, she would've liked to clear the air; one way or another. It wouldn't do either of them any good to leave things hanging—*unresolved*.

Lan stood a little way apart from the rest of the group, continuing to stare out through the Hangar windows and off across the lunar plains. It was almost impossible for her to imagine how things would be when she finally left the Moon behind for the last time; when she decided that the time was right for her to return to Earth.

The Moon would only ever exist for her in photographs—*in video*—at one remove; the only way the vast majority of the world would ever be allowed to witness it.

But at least she would have her memories.

Still beaming, the General checked on his Link. He blinked once—*twice*—and then turned to the mother. "Running a touch behind schedule," he said. "Gotta shake a leg." He glanced to his son, and then to Gofreddo. "You wouldn't mind if *Junior* here takes a look around the place; if he gets an eyeful of these wonderful *machines* you got here?"

Gofreddo looked to Lan, then said, "Actually, to tell the truth, I've got an appointment myself. You mind if I run these two back over to the Grand?" He dropped his voice a notch, but the boy—the General's son—seemed to be otherwise occupied, inspecting some aspect of the Shuttle's exterior in close-up detail. "You mind doing some babysitting?"

Lan shook her head. "That's fine," she said, and then she immediately regretted what she'd signed up for. She had been planning on heading to the gym; maybe to take another dip in the pool.

Oh, well, she supposed she'd have to put up with all her random thoughts till she could get her arms lifting—her legs *pumping*.

"Thanks," Gofreddo said, with a slight smile. Then he turned to the mother and father, and escorted them off out of the Hangar.

Lan felt herself and the boy watching them closely as they proceeded up the stairs and then out through the door to the PEAR landing strip.

All of a sudden, Lan felt somewhat self-conscious to find herself alone with the boy.

She had never been one of those people who was good with kids, or *animals* for that matter.

She was thoroughly stumped for what to say before she settled on the most obvious. "Has your dad got a meeting?"

The boy continued to examined the Shuttle's bodywork, getting himself down so close that his eyeball was almost touching it. To begin with, Lan thought the boy was actively ignoring her; that he was going to pull some *kid* trick on her. But then, right when she was certain he *wasn't* going to communicate, he turned and glanced over his shoulder. "That's classified," he said.

Lan took in his stern look; so similar to the one which seemed to be his father—*the General's*—default expression. It sent a shimmer through her gut.

Finally, right when it seemed like the tension in the room was weighing down the two of them, the boy cracked a smile. He snorted a laugh through his nose as if he had been attempting to keep it bottled away and only now—*reluctantly*—allowed it to be released into the Wider World.

Although Lan really couldn't tell what they were laughing about, she joined in.

She gave a nervous, overly girly giggle.

While she was thinking of something else to say, the boy beat her to it.

He walked his way slowly along the Shuttle, his eyes fixed upon the bodywork. "You know, I'm the only kid in my class who's got to go to the Moon."

It wasn't a question—no invitation for Lan's involvement.

It was just a *statement*.

The boy reached the end of the Shuttle and then continued, "Dad wants me to join up with the Army when I'm old enough—but I want to be an astronaut." He glanced back over his shoulder, almost as if he was testing Lan out—seeing if she'd laugh at him.

But she wasn't laughing.

And, what was more, she had *no intention* of laughing.

The boy sucked in a large amount of air, then he shifted his attention back onto the Shuttle. "I know I should feel good about this," he said. "I *know* that I should be making the most of this experience."

Lan couldn't help but sense his father—*the General's*—voice sneaking into his tone right there.

But she said nothing.

The boy continued, "But dad . . . I don't know . . . we're so *different*." He shook his head, then rounded the nose of the Shuttle so that he shifted out of sight.

Lan waited for the boy to emerge on the other side.

But he remained hidden.

Beginning to feel uneasy about the boy's absence—all too conscious of the fact that she was responsible for the boy's welfare—she trod her way up to the Shuttle, and then followed in his footsteps; approaching the last place she had seen him.

When Lan found him, the boy was huddled up, sitting on the ground, back against the Shuttle, his knees tucked into his chest. Tears rolled freely down his cheeks. And his eyes were red raw.

It sent a *pang* through Lan's blood.

Her first reaction was to look around.

To see if there might be someone to help her with this situation.

She had *never* been good with people like this . . . with *criers*.

In the end, it was when the boy brought his hands up to his face to hide his tears that Lan forced herself out of inaction. She stepped toward him, with no idea of what she was going to do. She was just allowing herself to act; no longer attempting to block away the emotions she'd felt all through her childhood, but, apparently like this boy, been scolded into hiding.

She crouched down beside him, her eyes still fixed onto his face, but keeping herself far enough away so that he had room.

Through his spread hands covering his face, the boy said, "Don't tell my dad about this . . . okay?"

Despite the boy's obviously distraught state, he kept his voice remarkably firm and even. She wondered if this wasn't borne out of practice. If the boy had had several opportunities to lock himself away in his bedroom with his tears.

Lan knew that *she* had.

She allowed a silence to envelope them.

Then she found something to say.

"You know, it all ends eventually." She drew in a deep breath, down into her lungs. "One way or another." She thought about going into more detail, but decided against it.

Everyone was different.

Each person's *journey* was different.

And she wouldn't allow herself to *presume* just how this boy's relations with his father would turn out. Hadn't she heard that somewhere? *Read* that somewhere?

. . . Perhaps while leafing through a parenting manual while she was bored . . .

They remained there—*together*—for what might've been only a few minutes, or as much as an hour. When Lan heard a cough from above, she flinched, then turned her attention in the direction of the sound. She saw someone coming through the Hangar doorway.

It took her a second or so to realise who it was.

Patrick Fourie.

VIP TREATMENT

*T*he *PEAR's visor* whirred shut, sealing Lan inside with Patrick.

As the PEAR's underpowered engine thrust them up into the air, Lan took in the Lunar Grand as it retreated from their vision. Such an enormous building—one which dominated the entirety of the Celestial Stays Dome's skyline. Her attention centred on the General's son—*Bernard*, as he'd revealed his name to be—as he stood on the staircase leading up to the Lunar Grand lobby.

He was waving to her.

Lan waved back at him, feeling a strange warmth developing in her gut.

It was weird.

She felt as if they'd made a connection.

Almost as if she'd been reaching through space and time to her former self—to who she had been in a previous life.

Soon after Patrick had shown up, Lan had received a message through her Link—*from Mackenzie Angliss, HR Supervisor*—that the

General's son was to be returned to the Lunar Grand; that some provision or other had been made for him.

While Patrick had observed the two of them—Bernard and Lan —he had appeared cool, detached. For the first time since it had occurred, Lan was glad for the impromptu 'chat' she'd had with Alicia. It had allowed her to know the reason why.

He was working out just what Lan's *angle* was.

The only thing was that Lan didn't have any 'angle'.

. . . Other than the attraction she'd felt.

The strange, unshakeable urge to follow up on what the kiss between them had started.

Wishing to lighten the atmosphere in the PEAR, Lan turned on Patrick.

He looked just as she recalled him—chiselled jawline; tightly packed muscles; and that almond-shaded, strawberry-blond hair.

"I wanted to talk to you about Kyra," Lan said, her voice firmer than she might've expected.

Especially after she'd gone and raked up all those painful past memories; the ones which'd concerned her own parents.

She didn't want to think about them anymore.

She *wouldn't* think about them anymore.

Patrick continued to stare forward.

Lan took the fact that he didn't reject her out of hand—didn't signal for the PEAR to come to a sudden standstill—that he was willing to hear her out.

So she continued.

"Kyra needed to tell me something." She paused, realising that she wouldn't be able to open up the way she would like—at least not yet. She was certain that Patrick noted her slight hesitation. But she tried to put it out of her mind. "Something *important*," Lan continued. "But it came out of the blue . . . we're not *friends*."

Lan felt a slight chill pass through her blood to hear her make that first remark.

And, for the first time, she realised just how seriously she felt about Patrick.

That she was willing to toss away another person so easily.

As if they were *nothing* to her.

. . . And yet the gratitude she felt toward Kyra remained.

She knew that.

She *knew* that.

Patrick remained sitting still, continuing to stare out through the visor at the lunar plains as the PEAR made rampant progress; as it trucked them over the landscape. Then, right when Lan was certain he wouldn't say another word to her—not ever again—he said, "It's okay; I think I knew that. I think I *realised* that." He turned side-on and examined her. "You don't worm your way into Gofreddo Zito's inner circle without having an impeccable sense of intuition about people."

Although Lan would beat herself up later for saying it, she couldn't help but allow it to slip out. "You mean like Alicia?"

Alicia, as they both well knew, was the one who had allowed Kyra to get close; the one who had *allowed* Gofreddo to be betrayed.

Lan felt her stomach crunch up on itself.

But Patrick appeared unmoved.

In fact, a faint smile appeared at the corner of his mouth.

Another silence settled upon them.

This time, though, it wasn't anywhere near as uncomfortable as the last one had been.

It was an almost *friendly* silence.

Lan felt almost loath to break it.

But she did.

"Where to now?" Lan asked.

The faint smile still lining his lips, Patrick said, "I was thinking of hitting the gym." His slightly nasal South African accent was beginning to sound familiar to Lan's ear.

Somewhere within her brain, Lan knew, there was some process or procedure absorbing the information surrounding that accent; tucking it away for later.

For when that recognition would prove useful.

When she might need to pin someone down to a specific place, or location, or time; like she had done with the General and his family.

He turned to her.

And she saw, once more, the flames in his eyes.

"That sound good to you?"

"Oh yes."

BIOMECHANICAL MANOEUVRES

*L*an *had to admit* that she had been surprised at first
—*surprised* at how easily Patrick kept up with her. She was
used to tucking herself away into some corner of the gym;
to losing herself to whatever routine she'd outlined for herself that
particular day. She always imagined herself as being miles ahead of
anyone else . . . although she hardly so much as glanced up to see
who might be working out beside her. Whenever she came to the
gym, it was to forget her surroundings.

And to forget what was going on within her brain.

Now, though, she had to admit that she was finding it difficult
—*very difficult indeed*—to keep her mind on anything *but* her
surroundings.

They'd hit the treadmills to begin the workout, and, as Lan had
imagined might well happen, they'd started into an unplanned
race. The two of them striving to one up the other in terms of
speed and distance run.

Patrick had come out on top in that particular encounter,

though—*granted*—there hadn't been any small amount of cheating involved. When the Link had called upon them to stop running—the personal timer they'd set expiring; signalling the end of the race—Patrick had taken the opportunity to continue his run for a good five or ten seconds.

So that he might just nudge himself ahead.

When they'd hit the weights, though, it'd been a different story altogether.

Lan had to admit that her gamesmanship had come out to play then.

Still hurting a little from the unfair loss of the previous competition, Lan had resolved that she was going to do nothing but *crush* Patrick in the next one.

She had feigned fear at the sight of the weights before settling for a pair of one-kilo dumbbells; the kinds that an older person might take along on a walk. It had been a risk; she didn't know how closely Patrick had paid attention to her previous visits to the gym . . . because if he had indeed paid attention at all then he would surely know that she was out to con him.

That she had her eye on the prize and she was determined not to be beaten.

Of course, Patrick had started off with a pair of far more respectable ten-kilo dumbbells, and Lan had watched on with faked astonishment as he'd laid himself down on the weight bench and begun to go through his reps.

She had bided her time, waited him out; waited until she saw the first film of sweat appear on his brow. And then she took her opportunity to strike.

With the same wide-eyed, doe-like expression on her face—or so Lan pictured herself—she went over to the dumbbells and selected a pair just like Patrick's.

A pair of ten-kilos.

Red-faced, beads of sweat rolling down his face, Patrick had looked on with an expression approaching concern. For a second, she thought that he might lift himself up off the weight bench and stop her from going through with what she planned.

Not wanting her to *hurt* herself . . .

But, instead, he stayed his ground, apparently content to watch what was going to play out.

Taking up the weight bench alongside Patrick, Lan started into the first few repetitions. It wasn't too difficult for her to show strain on her face to begin with because she felt the remainder of the side injury bothering her. But, once she got into the swing of the reps, she decided to allow her poker face to drop. And for Patrick to see what he was *really* up against.

She shot through the repetitions, lifting hundreds of times before she even began to feel herself tiring. And then she forced herself onward; determined to show him her true strength.

When she was finally done with the dumbbells, she turned to him—he had gone a pale shade—and she casually asked him to hand her a pair of the twenty-five kilo dumbbells, so that she could lift some 'real' weight.

Although Patrick was clearly stunned by the whole show playing out before his eyes, he did as she said, handing them over to her. When she glanced up at him, she saw that he was more *curious* than anything else to see if she could really lift so much weight consistently.

And she *sure* showed him . . .

Once they'd got done with the weight-training session, and with Patrick still wearing a look of extreme shock, Lan beckoned him over to the exercise bikes; where they were right now. They had chosen a pair of bikes alongside one another. If this was to be the deciding round of whatever it was they were duking out in the gym, then Lan was determined to be the victor.

Even as she clambered onto the saddle, Lan felt somewhat apprehensive.

She was hurting more than she was going to admit.

Her left side was really stinging now.

More than anything it annoyed her—was there anything more annoying than pain?

She had thought she'd got over the injury in the course of the past few days. She wondered if she should head to the Infirmary; get a doctor to have a look at her. It wasn't that she was afraid of medicine, or doctors—she had no irrational fears like those—it was more a case of not having time to get around to it. Perhaps that was another lesson which her parents had subconsciously hammered into her throughout her childhood; that there wasn't anything as self-indulgent as being concerned about yourself . . .

Lan had quickly learned what a folly that was; that if she didn't make looking after herself a matter of great importance then she would only eventually become dependent on someone else to look after her. This, though—this *competition* she was going through with Patrick—it demanded that she just work on through the pain barrier.

She wasn't going to lose face.

Not now.

They cut through the bullshit, deciding once and for all that they were entering a competition.

Leaning over into her bike, smelling intoxicatingly of sweat and musk, Patrick said, "We'll make it ten klicks, huh?"

Lan jabbed her finger into her earpiece, setting that distance as the goal. When she glanced back at him, she saw that he was going through the same procedure.

As he turned back to his bike, Patrick smiled to himself. *"High resistance, okay? Level Ten."*

Lan winced, and immediately scolded herself for doing so.

She wasn't supposed to show any emotion.

Not while she was in competition.

Not while she was trying to *win*.

She went through the procedure; having the Link set the parameters which Patrick had defined.

Level Ten was the toughest incline the bikes would handle.

To be honest, Lan never really ventured much beyond Level Five or Six; she didn't use exercise bikes for anything other than the cooldown portion of her workout routine.

From the looks of Patrick, she could see that he was gearing up for some serious sprinting; that he was going to leap up this imaginary hill.

She prepared herself.

Breathed in deeply.

Felt the sharp pain in her side.

"Go!" Patrick said, all at once standing up in his pedals.

Lan punched hard against the pedals, using the balls of her feet —the technique which she had been taught from an early age was the most energy-efficient way to propel herself forward on a bike. To build up momentum, she had to sink her weight down on the right pedal, and then the left, and then the *right* . . . already she could feel her whole body tensing; her power moving through her right side, and then her left . . . and that was when the pain came in.

But, as she'd done before, she pushed it away.

Refused to acknowledge it.

For the first time in their joint venture into the gym, she ceased to notice Patrick.

He became only part of the scenery.

She supposed—if it hadn't been for the pain—she might've had an opportunity to acknowledge the Zenlike, thoughtless state which she entered. She might've had the opportunity to *enjoy* it . . . but there was so much pain.

As she forced herself onward—forced herself *up* the hill—she felt something in her left side snap. It happened suddenly, and when it did she felt all the force leave her body; all her strength *desert* her . . . and—just like that—she felt herself topple forward.

Then down.

Onto the floor.

URGENT ATTENTION

*T*he lights in the Infirmary corridors were almost too bright for Patrick to stand.

It reminded him of when he would go out on an extended trip across the lunar plains—when all the lights in the Shuttle would be down; with only the multi-coloured illuminated instrument panels to see by. It was upon returning, as he brought the Shuttle in through the doors to the Hangar that he felt the overpowering strength of the light.

Dazzling him.

It all happened so quickly.

Patrick had hardly time to think.

One minute he was pressing himself onward, determined to reach the ten-kilometre mark he had set himself—and thus win the exercise-bike race—and then, the next, on hearing a hard *exhale* from beside him, he witnessed Lan tumbling off her own bike and falling to the floor.

He had leaped off his bike at once, of course.

And he tended to her as best he could.

He established quickly that she had passed out; that the heat, or the force of the exercise had got to her. She had been unable to take any more.

Someone had called for help, and a group of medics from the Infirmary had shown up in short order. In the panic, he had simply tagged along; becoming unaware of his sweaty clothing.

Or the fact that he could hardly walk straight after the exertion he'd put himself through.

Now that he stalked the Infirmary corridors, though, he could feel the incessant, rankling pain all through his body. It worked up the backs of his calves, lingering on the surface of his thighs. His stomach ached; his arms too. It'd been a long time since he'd *really* ached after a workout . . . and he knew that it was because he'd been trying to impress Lan.

As he stalked the Infirmary corridor something struck him.

That Lan had been trying to impress him *too*.

And now she was here.

Whenever Patrick spotted a passing medic, he stopped them, asked if there was any news of Lan Niu. And they told him, without exception, that nothing had changed about her condition. And that—*no*—he couldn't go into see her.

That she wasn't yet in a state which permitted her to have company.

Patrick didn't know what he should do.

He spurned the medics' suggestions that he should return to the Basements.

Get himself some rest.

And a *shower*.

He wouldn't feel right with himself if he did that.

He felt that he was *directly* responsible for what'd happened to her.

Finally—it must've been about two or three hours after she'd been admitted to the Infirmary—he collared a nearby medic who informed him that Lan had come around from the fainting spell she'd suffered. That she was conscious. And ready to receive visitors.

Patrick couldn't hold himself back. He rushed through the corridors, the lights a scattered flurry in his vision. He ploughed on through the door, and into Lan's room.

Just as the medic had claimed, she was sitting upright in bed.

She looked slightly faint.

A touch pale.

But she was conscious, and—*clearly*—responding.

She turned her head to him, and he caught her black eyes with his own.

His heart fluttered up to his throat.

And his pulse quickened.

He trod toward her bedside, and then suddenly felt timid, as if he didn't know what to do next.

As if he was *afraid* of what he should do next.

Patrick pushed away these fears . . . who was he trying to kid? He was a hell-for-leather Lunar Shuttle pilot; he pulled loop-the-loops for fun; he performed all manner of death-defying feats just because he enjoyed the way his stomach sank.

His stomach was sinking now.

As he reached out to take Lan's hand.

He rested his skin up against hers, feeling the warmth in her touch.

"How're you feeling?" he said.

Lan gave a shrug and a smile. A combination of gestures which could've meant just about anything. Then she said, "I had a cracked rib—that's what they found on the X-ray."

"Yeah?" Patrick replied.

Lan's smile transformed into a wry grin. "Yeah . . . but don't worry, it wasn't from that workout with you—it's a *past* injury. One which I didn't allow to heal properly."

Despite the situation—and against his relief that Lan was apparently recovering well—he couldn't help but feel a tightness across his chest. Just to think how much he'd seen her lifting . . . and that with a *cracked rib*? God knew what she'd be like when she had a clean bill of health.

Patrick's mind boggled for several moments.

Then he turned his attention back to Lan.

And he had another chance to appreciate just how beautiful she really was.

The medics had picked out her plaits so that her hair hung down loose, coiling about her waist.

The bedspread was drawn up to just below her breasts.

Lan looked at him, and then patted a spot on the bed. "Sit," she said.

Patrick hung back for another moment, and then, finally, he did as she said. "I'm sorry things turned out this way. I mean, with you in the *Infirmary*."

Thankfully Lan saw the humour in his ridiculous statement and she smiled widely. "Well, it's certainly some second date," she said.

Patrick smiled back at her, then drew breath. He looked down over himself, still wearing his tracksuit. "I guess I must be stinking up the place—probably better if I go back to the Basements, like those medics have been trying to make me do for the past few hours."

Lan didn't say anything to this.

"All right," Patrick said, getting to his feet, ready to leave Lan to recover.

He'd hardly taken more than two steps before he felt a strong hold on his arm.

He turned quickly.

Saw that—*somehow*—Lan had whipped back the bedcovers, that she had managed to reach out and grab him. If he ever had any need for her to back up her performance in the gym with more evidence of her superior physical prowess she was doing so right now.

"You know what?" she said.

"What?" Patrick replied, realising that he was trembling.

"There's an en suite shower here." She nodded in the direction of a door; adjoining the hospital room.

Patrick felt himself sinking.

And then, as if caught at the same instant, rising upward.

Impossibly quickly.

CLINICAL PRECISION

The warm water streamed down Lan's skin. She felt it working its way, first in rivulets, and then in torrents, down her back, down her navel . . . pouring down each of her legs.

Puddling at her feet.

Steam clung to the air making it hard to breathe.

Lan felt a steady throb of pain down at her left side—at where the medics had bandaged her up; where the medics had assured her she had cracked a rib. That bandage was gone, now, of course.

Feeling the warm steam rising all around her, she turned into Patrick.

He was tender; clearly concerned about harming her.

But he had no need to worry.

Whatever pain meds she'd been administered had made what had once been a sharp pain in her side only a distant memory. Only a half-remembered tingle.

Patrick's hands were smooth, and they moved effortlessly over her skin. Even through the warm steam, she felt his hot breath. She could feel his pulse up against her own.

Their hearts beating to the same rhythm.

Lan stood before him, her hair dripping wet, hanging down the middle of her back. She had seen him looking; seen his desperation to get his hands onto her hair . . . to allow it to run smooth between his fingers. Well, now was his chance. She was his now.

All his.

His body seemed to attract hers.

She reached out and pressed her fingertips against his bristling muscles.

They were *firm* . . . just like her own.

It made her smile slightly to think back to the gym.

Sure, it had ended badly, but she had shown him her strength.

Her *true* strength.

And she was ready to do so again.

Acting on impulse, she reached for his hands—his *curious* hands —and she wrestled hold of his wrists; holding them firmly in her grip. She pressed them hard against the bathroom tiles, feeling them make contact with the firm surface.

He gasped.

The water continued to fall.

It splashed about their feet.

About their naked bodies.

The lights were down low . . . Patrick had managed to locate a dimmer switch.

She had him right where she wanted him.

Right where she *needed* him.

Feeling all her strength becoming wrapped up in her arms, she maneuvered Patrick so that she pressed his back up against the tiles. She felt the warm water squirt over them. It sent waves of warmth through her blood. And the pain meds sent dizzying waves to her brain.

Or was it Patrick who sent the dizzying waves to her brain?

She couldn't tell any longer.

When she was sure that she had him under her control—that she had him pinned down; that he wouldn't be going anywhere in a hurry—she wrapped her legs about his waist, easing him into herself. She felt the warmth, and the strength, and the comfort from his arms which now embraced her . . . the arms which she had *allowed* loose.

Her whole body went rigid momentarily.

And then it became impossibly soft.

As if Patrick worked a calming influence over her.

As if he was *meant* for her.

But she'd never believed in any of that stuff. So why now?

She pushed all conscious thoughts to the periphery of her mind.

And she focussed on the sensations.

Only on the sensations.

Until she felt ready to burst.

21

WAKE-UP CALL

There was the sound of knocking at the door.

Lan stirred from the Infirmary bed.

She felt the warmth beside her. She turned.

Saw that it was Patrick lying there.

Duvet draped over him.

Sleeping soundlessly.

When Lan caught back hold of her senses, she realised that her Link had been prompting her to wake up for the past five minutes. That there was a series of unattended alerts. She attended to them now, shutting off each one in sequence. From behind the door, she heard a voice.

"Lan? Lan?"

A bolt ran up her spine.

A tingle through her belly.

She forced herself up and out of bed.

Realising that she was stark naked, she caught hold of the hospital gown which dangled off the back of a nearby chair. She shrugged it on over her shoulders and tried not to think too much about its curtailed length . . . how it left very little to the imagination.

When she reached the door, she paused, thought about what she was doing.

And then, hearing another hurried knock, she decided to open up.

If she didn't open up then someone might think she was in trouble and try to break the door right down. She *was* in a hospital room, after all. She was *supposed* to be in ill health.

Well, she *did* have a cracked rib, didn't she?

When she brought the door open, she found a pair of eyes staring back at her.

It took her another heartbeat to put the pieces of the puzzle together.

Alicia Brennan.

Louise Williams.

Although looking back on it—just about anything else would've been more appropriate—Lan couldn't help blurting out, "What're *you* doing here?"

It seemed even more rash when she turned her attention downward; to the item which Louise and Alicia bore between the two of them. A wicker basket with a tea towel to keep the contents warm . . . some—*no-doubt delicious*—baked treats of Alicia's devising.

Now that Lan thought about it, she was certain she could smell blueberry muffins. And, well, she had to admit that she could really do with a blueberry muffin about now. Her mind snapped back onto the perilousness of the situation.

"It's nice to see you too," Alicia said, her voice just as bouncy— as full as life—as it always seemed to be; day or night.

"Good to see you're out of bed," Louise said.

Lan glanced over her shoulder; back to Patrick, who continued to sleep away in the hospital bed. When she turned to Louise and Alicia, she knew that she must be blushing all over the place.

Indeed, the wide-eyed expressions—one from Louise; another from Alicia—confirmed their thoughts.

"Oh," Alicia said, taking a step back, then slipping Louise a side-long glance. "*Sorry.*"

Lan felt her chest tighten, and a touch of pain jangle through her ribs. All her muscles seemed to jerk tight for a long moment. She felt a great deal of discomfort. But she resisted the urge to wince.

Together, Alicia and Louise held out the wicker basket to Lan.

Lan hesitated for a long moment, suddenly unsure about what she should do; how she should act. Of course she was glad that Louise and Alicia had come here to see her; in so doing they'd shown more concern than she'd believed anyone would direct toward her current condition. Perhaps she'd been a tad hasty in writing off humankind. Then again, on the other hand, Lan really wanted to get shot of Louise and Alicia just as soon as possible. It was already gut-wrenchingly embarrassing that things had moved so quickly with Patrick, but to allow Louise and Alicia to know the truth—the *whole* truth—would be mortifying. Sure, they *assumed* she was 'entertaining' company, but they didn't know the full ins and outs of the thing . . . *yet.*

Lan took the wicker basket from Louise and Alicia, already feeling that warming, buttery scent of blueberry muffins sneaking its way up to her nostrils. "Thanks," she managed to get out through clenched teeth.

"Don't mention it," Alicia replied, with that same happy-go-lucky, girl-next-door tone.

Louise didn't say anything herself, but she did give Lan a particularly sweet smile.

When Alicia made to disappear off down the corridor, she turned back just before slipping around the corner. She mouthed a message which Lan—*unfortunately*—had no trouble decoding.

Tell me the details later!

Blushing even more, Lan turned back into the hotel room. She lowered herself onto the edge of the bed, the wicker basket containing the blueberry muffins beside her, and she looked across Patrick's face . . . his sleeping features.

She'd been watching him for only a few seconds when she noted the slight twitch of his eyelid, and the truth struck her right in the solar plexus. "You're *awake*, aren't you?"

Patrick remained still another few moments as if he might be able to deny pure facts by just putting on a good act. But she had already rumbled him. Finally, apparently willing to give himself up, he slowly opened his eyelids, those gorgeous hazel irises glinting in the light, like flakes of bronze. He gave a faux yawn, then said, "I miss something?"

Acting on impulse, and forgetting her cracked rib for the time being, Lan reached across and gave him a punch on the upper arm.

He flinched at the blow.

Sunk his teeth into his lower lip.

He only remained somewhat injured by the experience momentarily; his wincing expression soon replaced by a wicked smile. He nodded to the wicker basket. "And what've we got there?"

Shifting her body so that she placed herself between Patrick and the basket, Lan said, "That's none of your business—*Alicia* baked them for me . . ." She arched an eyebrow then nodded to the door. "The medic will be making the morning rounds before too long; I'd get yourself shot of here before then . . . you wouldn't want to find yourself getting into trouble with Mackenzie Angliss, now, would you?"

Although Patrick did his best to hide his immediate reaction to Lan mentioning Mackenzie Angliss's name, Lan caught the sudden shock . . . or had it been *horror*? . . . which crossed his features. She would have to think on that.

All the same—*whatever the real reason*—Patrick quickly shifted out from beneath the duvet, casting it to the floor. He hurriedly dressed himself in the sweaty tracksuit he had arrived to the Infirmary in yesterday. "Shit," he said, apparently checking his Link. "It's *late* . . . I'm going to be late for duty."

"You'd better shake a leg then," Lan replied, knowingly parroting the expression the General had used the day before.

Sometimes she wondered what she might do with the space freed up by all the next-to-useless English idioms she stored in her brain. Probably nothing of substance . . .

Patrick was readying to leave the room when Lan decided she should give him just a little mercy.

She called him back.

He turned to her.

Seemed to realise—*instinctively*—what was wrong.

Lan pursed her lips, and Patrick leaned down into her. The kiss began as something soft, romantic; a mere pressing of their lips together. But it soon evolved into *so* much more.

By the time they were through, Lan found her breathing coming shallow.

And it wasn't because of her cracked rib.

When they finally broke apart, Lan felt as if she'd left something of herself with Patrick. As if, while Patrick made his way to the door, he was taking a part of her out with him.

Once the door slid shut behind him, she found herself alone.

Alone in the hospital room.

Then—*and only then*—did she begin to feel the gentle, throbbing pain at her left side.

Hopefully the medics would be by soon with some pills.

SHORT CIRCUIT

*L*an *checked out* of the Infirmary later that morning. When the doctor looked her over, she made no small matter of the redness which'd appeared across her abdomen overnight. Lan had to exercise no small amount of restraint to keep from smiling . . . to keep from revealing that the swelling was a result of something very much apart from the cracked rib.

The doctor had given her some pills to take for the pain—along with some others which were supposed to help with the swelling.

Lan took both sets of pills right down, and turned her mind to the day ahead.

The doctor had granted her *light* duty for the day, which meant that she should report as usual to Duval; that she should take her orders from him, but with the provision that she was not to be taking part in any heavy lifting or shootouts until she had had a chance to recover.

Lan was certain that 'light' duty would be her one-way ticket back to a desk, so she was pleasantly surprised that—when she called in to receive her day's orders from Duval—he informed her that she would be heading out to the Armstrong Archive that morning . . . that she would be working security with a fellow team member.

Dutifully, Lan flagged down the nearest PEAR and floated off to the far end of the Celestial Stays Dome. When she arrived, she wasn't surprised to find that the Archive was more or less empty.

There was one thing which she'd grasped throughout her employment with Celestial Stays, and that was that people didn't tend to pay to come all the way to the Moon so that they might sit about; poring over texts or staring at images.

Soon enough, Lan found herself alone in the Archive lobby.

When she went to the desk, rang the buzzer there, Miguel Cruz emerged from some back room. As always—as he *always* appeared to Lan—he had five o'clock shadow and more than the suggestion of a hangdog look about him. His eyes, though, glinted out from above the glasses he was currently wearing perched on the tip of his nose. He gave Lan a slight smile, and she found herself momentarily distracted by the sprawling tattoo which rose up his neck, and which seemed to extend down the collar of his overalls, and beyond. "Can I help you?" he asked.

Lan absorbed his slightly Spanish-accented English. Then she flipped past the detail; discarding it from her mind for the time being. "I've been posted here," she said. "There should be another member of the Security Division already here."

Miguel pouted then shrugged. "You must mean Doug," he said. "He doesn't usually get here till a little later." Here Miguel cracked a slight smile. "Seems to think that he can afford to get in a few extra hours' sleep—that if the invasion does come then the Armstrong Archive will be the very least of the invaders' concerns."

Lan smiled slightly at this oddball joke, then said, "What does *security* even entail here—at the Archive?"

Miguel set his palms down on the desk between the two of them, showing off his muscular forearms. Lan could tell that he lifted weights too. She recalled seeing him a few times at the gym.

"When someone comes in I'll give you a buzz on the Link," he said, pointing to his own neural implant. "Other than that the job —as far as my *non-Security* trained eye goes—is just to wander about the place keeping a look out on things."

"Okay, thanks," Lan said, stepping away from the desk.

As Miguel returned into whatever back room he'd emerged from, Lan padded her way up the stairs leading into the Archive. She thought to herself about how Duval might not have put her on a desk, but he had certainly given her the very lightest of *light* duties available beneath the Dome.

She wasn't sure what to make of it . . . did he really think that she was so down-and-out that she couldn't do her job like normal? It rankled her to show weakness and she silently cursed the doctor for having made her condition public; for having gone out of her way to contact *Lan's* superior to inform him of what she was—*and wasn't*—capable of.

Then again, she wondered if she might not be able to prove herself here; at the Archive.

Trouble sometimes started up in the unlikeliest of places.

Lan had reached the opposite end of the Archive and was staring out of the window when she thought to do a time check. She realised that an hour had passed. When she glanced back over her shoulder, she observed all the stacks; all of the physical books, and all of the assorted media. She recalled having read about the Archive acting as some kind of failsafe for human records back on Earth . . . that if some sort of an apocalyptic scenario came to pass

Earthside—and all human records were somehow destroyed—a skeleton set of records would be preserved on Luna. So that the survivors might rebuild. If there were any survivors at all.

As she peered out across the lunar plains, not thinking about anything much in particular—and not *wanting* to think about anything much in particular—she heard a familiar voice.

"Lan?"

She turned to see that, sure enough, Kyra was standing on her heels.

Her pretty, delicate features, and her smooth, walnut-coloured skin.

As always, she wore her sleek, nut-brown hair up in a bun.

That same look of innocence lingered about her face.

Appearances, Lan knew well, could be deceiving.

At least that was what everyone *said* about Kyra.

Try as she might—even after the conversation with Alicia; the 'serious' chat they'd shared—Lan couldn't summon any feelings of anger against her.

After all, Kyra had never done anything against *Lan*.

"Hi," Lan said, turning her back on the lunar plains, and finding her tone of voice coming across as much lighter than she would've expected . . . much *jollier* than she would've expected.

Perhaps it was the pills; or that she bore Kyra no ill will; or perhaps—*just perhaps*—it was because of what'd happened last night. Not the cracked ribs . . . the *other* thing . . .

"I was looking for you all over." Kyra tilted her head backward, apparently to indicate the entrance to the Armstrong Archive. "I just happened to drop in here, and I got talking to Miguel who said there was a new member of the Security Division who'd shown up, then of course he told me it was you, and . . ."

Kyra allowed her words to drift off into nothing.

Lan took this as her cue to pick up the conversation. "Do you have more information about my parents? About what they're *up* to?"

Kyra pouted for a second, then looked past Lan and out the window. She lingered a long time on the lunar plains, losing herself—as Lan had done so many times—in the hypnotic patterns of the craters and the dust. "No," she replied. "I don't have any more information on them."

"Then what did you want to see me about?" Lan replied, realising, right away, that she'd allowed her daisy-fresh tone to drop; and that it'd been replaced by a no-nonsense, route-one approach to conversation.

Kyra turned her attention back onto Lan. "I was . . . well, I was *speaking* with Frau Köhler recently, and we agreed that it might be a good idea to profile the various Divisions beneath the Celestial Stays Dome . . . to get to know the people on the ground; those who provide such a . . . uh . . . an *exclusive* service to its guests."

Although it was subtle, Lan noted Kyra's pause; she noted that Kyra had hesitated so that she might search for the appropriate word. She supposed that—like most other employees beneath the Dome—Kyra had a envy issues when it came to the exclusive, almost unfalteringly wealthy clientele of Celestial Stays.

"So . . ." Lan said, allowing the word to linger. "What does this have to do with me?"

Kyra blinked a couple of times, and Lan admitted that she felt bad for the tone she was striking.

But what could she do?

This was just her natural way of *speaking* . . .

Some people had a way with others while Lan simply *didn't* . . .

"Well," Kyra replied, sounding more than a little knocked back now, "I was wondering if you would be the member of the Security

Division that I could interview." She glanced up at Lan, met her eye, and tried out a cautionary smile. "If you wouldn't have a problem with it."

Lan waited out the seconds, wondering if there might be a thinly veiled threat lurking. Kyra had invoked Frau Köhler's name once already in the conversation, and she wondered if she would do it again; implying that Lan might fall out of favour with her boss if she didn't bend to her whim.

It was an unnatural position for Lan, to tell the truth, since she could never rightly say that she *had* ever bent to the whim of a boss. Whenever Lan had had a boss like that—a boss who had attempted to take liberties—she would simply pack up her things and move onto the next job.

That wasn't such an easy option now that she was on the Moon, though.

Lan thought another moment or so, and realised, for good or ill, that the charm offensive—or whatever she should call it—that Alicia had pulled on her was the reason for her icy tone toward Kyra. Why was she allowing Alicia to dictate what she should do?

Why should she allow *anyone* to dictate what she should do?

Resolved now, she turned to Kyra. "Okay," she said, with a slight smile, feeling somewhat wicked about accepting even knowing that she had every right to do so.

23

EARTHSIDE CONCERNS

Jié Niu peered out through the chilled glass of her apartment. She looked down onto Huashan Park. She watched several warmly dressed joggers trotting their way along the path. In the early-morning air, their exhalations caused mist to form about their mouths and nostrils. None of them ran in pairs; all of them ran alone. Each of them on their own separate journey. All of them carrying their own motivation. Some days Jié found herself speculating what these motivations might be; but, this morning, she had little room for speculation or any other grand imaginative efforts.

She had been up half the night, and even when she had managed to drift off to sleep it was only to wake up again moments later . . . imagining that a *creak* she heard out in the hallway—a *tapping* sound against the window—might be the sign of someone about to break in. Of course it was ridiculous to believe that someone would be able to come in through the window. The apartment—the one in which she and her husband,

Yŏng, had lived all their married lives—was located on the twenty-second floor of the building.

Then again, it seemed ridiculous to think someone might attempt to kidnap their daughter. And yet that was what intelligence had told them; the branch of the Chinese government they had enlisted to help track their daughter, Lan.

Jié had been the one to receive the news. It had been just like any other day. She had gone into the office which she cherished, and, as was her custom when she closed the door behind her, she'd run her fingertips along the pristine, oak shelf on her way to her desk.

When she had sat down, she had felt somehow different.

Although Jié had never been the superstitious kind—*that would've been more in keeping with her countryside family*—she had felt something . . . nothing more than the rising of a few hairs at the back of her neck; a pinching of the skin at the tender inner-flesh of her upper arms.

She had almost convinced herself it was a ghost.

That a *ghost* was reaching out to her from the Nether . . . trying to tell her something.

When she had signed onto her Link, the message had been there waiting.

The one which explained the plot.

And which had proposed a variety of solutions.

From the kitchen, Jié could smell the tender scent of the baking baozi; the buns she had set to cook in the early hours of the morning. That was one of those antiquated habits which she had never been able to shake. It was her mother's influence. Although she knew that Yŏng would be delighted—not to mention *surprised*—to find the baked treats awaiting him for breakfast, she hadn't done it out of some wish to please her husband. She had baked the baozi just to breathe in the smell. To calm her uneasy stomach.

Feeling a creeping chill—a draught—sneak up the hem of her *shanqun* robe, she pulled the sash tighter about her waist. The silk felt sleek, but it caused her to sweat more than instilling warming waves beneath her skin. She wondered if she should drape a blanket about her shoulders. That might take care of the cold. But she could hardly gather the strength to move.

Her gaze remained fixed on the park below.

Within the apartment, she could hear Yǒng stirring. No doubt, as was his wont, he was padding the bed, searching for her, wishing to drape his arm across her sleeping form.

And, no doubt, he had realised that she wasn't there.

When she had been younger Jié had often found herself worried about something—*concerned for some reason*. She had often sought out some confidante so that she might talk the matter over.

Now, though—*now that she had made Brigadier General in the ROCAF*—she had witnessed her options rapidly diminishing. She had realised this very night, waking in a cold sweat, that there was absolutely nobody on the planet with whom she would feel comfortable talking this issue over. It was no use to speak with Yǒng, of course, he would only become exasperated as he attempted to *fix* the matter. It had been under his guidance that they had gone with the plan to release a story—through Chinese media—about their daughter being killed on the trip to the Moon . . . while she was en route to taking up a contract with Celestial Stays.

It sent a pang through Jié's heart to imagine Lan's reaction when she read those articles. But she had been assured by knowledgeable sources that those in Celestial Stays's employ had their access to media severely restricted. Indeed, it was this knowledge which kept Jié from hating herself for what she and her husband had done.

The story had bought them time.

At least that was what their sources had told them.

It would assuage the kidnappers for the time being.

And, after all, could their daughter have chosen a safer place to hide than the Moon?

It would be a tough preposition indeed for them to reach her there!

Hearing her husband's footsteps out in the corridor behind her, Jié tilted her head slightly in the direction of the sound. She wanted nothing but to be alone now—*alone* with her thoughts. Sometimes she couldn't help wondering if she wouldn't have been better treading a path similar to that of her daughter . . . casting off the shackles of her society—of her *expectations*—and venturing out into the world alone.

Just to think of Lan sent another pan through her stomach.

It had been Jié's decision to allow Lan to come around in her own good time; for Lan to have the opportunity of reaching out to *them* . . . her parents. She had been strict with Yŏng whenever he had wished to make the first move; to reach out and contact her. And it had only been with Jié's perennial reprimand that he had obeyed her; that he had seen that if they backed down then they might well lose Lan forever. It was true that it had been the best part of fifteen years since they had seen their daughter—and it would've been a lie to say that it *didn't* hurt every day—but they had kept a watchful eye on her. They had always been looking out for her . . . following her tracks.

Allowing her the illusion of independence.

This was the first time when they had been compelled to act.

And Jié couldn't help wondering if she might not regret it for the rest of her life.

As she felt Yǒng's gentle footsteps sound his approach, she stared down across the park below, watching the joggers going round and round and *round* again. She couldn't help wondering if they were trying to lose their minds through mindless repetition. Jié couldn't help wondering if that wasn't what she'd been attempting to achieve for the entirety of her life.

Attempting and *failing*.

24

DOWNTIME

Patrick always felt at a loose end whenever a free day cropped up on his calendar. This time, though, he had to admit that he felt somewhat more anxious than usual. Whereas he tended to go down the Stellar Tide Casino—perhaps take part in a few of the lower-stakes card games—he found that he couldn't quite bring himself to enjoy such base diversions today.

The night before, when he'd been winding down, he'd discovered the worst case of Gofreddo's neglect so far.

Patrick had gone through the well-worn ritual. And, as had often been the case over the previous weeks, he had taken special care with his inspections; knowing that there would surely be *something* that Gofreddo had neglected to take care of.

Once Patrick had got through with the cursory inspection of the Shuttle's underside, going through the monotonous checks of the wires—making sure there weren't any burned-out or melted components—he had found nothing amiss.

And so he had switched his attention to the Shuttle itself.

To the interior.

When he had trod his way up the steps, he had felt something like apprehension tightening up his shoulders; making him feel tense.

He knew the feeling had struck him because he was *waiting* to find the problem.

Not wondering if there *might* be a problem.

Because he knew there would be . . .

He got through with checking over the passenger seats, and he was pleasantly surprised to see that all the chest straps—the safety harnesses—were in place. That there appeared to be no superficial issues. Once he'd got through with the seats, he ventured on into the cockpit.

And that had been where he'd located the problem.

It had stared Patrick in the face.

So *clear* that Patrick could hardly believe what he was seeing.

Gofreddo had left the Shuttle computer switched on.

Now, while this wouldn't ordinarily have been any big issue, it would only have been a matter of flipping it off, after all; Patrick saw that not only had Gofreddo left the ship's computer switched on, but he had left the Control Panel *initiated*. This meant that, at the touch of the screen, anybody might've been able to engage the thrusters. Anyone—*not knowing what they were doing*—might've flamed up the engines and sent the Shuttle spiralling out of control through the exit to the Hangar.

There was no doubt about the seriousness of the matter.

If it had been Patrick who'd been involved—and his neglect had been discovered and reported—he would've been unceremoniously tossed right back to Earth.

And not without good reason.

This level of neglect could potentially not only put the Shuttle and its occupants in danger; but, if the pilot hit the steering just the wrong way, the whole Celestial Stays Dome.

It wouldn't take a large blow against the Dome to pierce the protective wall.

And to kill everyone within.

Patrick had decided that this time he needed to take action. And, since he no longer trusted himself to confront Gofreddo about the issue, he had decided he had no option but to go above both their heads. Gofreddo might well be his best friend, but when several hundred people's lives were at risk, friendship had to be put in perspective.

Having taken the entire night to think the matter through—to see if he might *possibly* be able to suck up the courage to confront Gofreddo with the issue himself—Patrick had made an appointment this morning to meet with Mackenzie Angliss. Although she had prompted him for a subject, apparently so she could prioritise him as necessary, he had only told her that it was an *urgent* matter. That allowed Patrick the option of backing out at the last moment.

Of not saying anything at all.

But now, as Patrick rose up in the lift to one of the upper floors of the Lunar Grand—where Mackenzie kept her office—he found himself peering out across the whole of the Celestial Stays Dome below him and he knew that he had to do the right thing.

That he couldn't *knowingly* put hundreds of people's lives in danger.

As he disembarked the lift, he supposed that it was something of a testament to Gofreddo Zito's charm that he had managed to keep Patrick from spilling the beans for so long; that he had managed to keep Patrick from *reporting* on him.

Mackenzie's office was wall-to-wall glass, which afforded those approaching a no-holds barred view into her room. To whatever she might be doing.

Right then, Mackenzie Angliss appeared to Patrick just as she always did within his mind's eye. Her finger stuck in her earpiece as she sent off some message or other via her neural implant.

When she noticed him, she gave him a vague smile and a finger-wiggle of a wave. Then she shifted her attention back to whatever instruction she was sending off through the Link, turning away from him, looking out the window, down across the Celestial Stays Dome spread before her.

As Patrick drew closer still, he had the opportunity to absorb her appearance:

Red hair.

Green eyes.

Tanned skin.

In some other life she might've been a supermodel; for all Patrick really knew about Mackenzie, she might well have been one, back down on Earth. And, just like a supermodel, there was something about her which had never quite made her seem *real* to him. Some *photogenic* untouchable quality about her. He supposed to have arrived in the position where she had arrived within Celestial Stays—*Supervisor of Human Resources*—she had had to keep her distance from others . . . especially looking the way she did.

Patrick supposed that she had had several opportunities to use her looks to get what she wanted in business, but, at least to his mind, she had got ahead through subtler merits; chief among those her work ethic. There was much to admire in Mackenzie. She was certainly a *damn sight* more successful than he could claim to be.

Patrick hovered outside the door to her office for several seconds, knowing that this was his chance to turn back; that he could make some excuse, claim that he had been *overthinking* some issue. But, no, now he had come this far his reasoning *had* to be solid, if not entirely flawless.

For him to go this far down the path to betraying Gofreddo —*his best friend*—it had to be something irretrievably important.

Mackenzie turned, nodded for him to come in.

25

INVESTIGATIONAL DUTIES

Lan and Kyra sat on one of the upper floors of the Armstrong Archive. It was several days into Lan's role at the Archive; it seemed that the doctor had continued to advise her superior, Duval, that she was still only suited for 'light' duties. To tell the truth, Lan did feel quite significant pain from the cracked rib—she certainly wouldn't be back to her normal gym routine for a while yet, although the pills had helped her to get through the days without too much trouble.

Sleeping was another matter entirely, though.

Several times, she'd woken in the middle of the night, finding herself having returned to her standard sleeping position; lying on her stomach. Whenever she first awoke it was like a gentle, prickling pain in her chest. But it soon graduated into a searing, hot unbearable sensation.

And that was where the pills came in.

"Go back to the beginning," Kyra said, glancing up over the

screen she was working with; the device with which she was taking audio and written notes.

Lan drew in a sharp breath. Then she peered out through the window, and across the lunar plains which stretched out beyond the glass. She really didn't know how to feel about this situation.

Didn't know how *comfortable* she felt about it.

When Kyra had first floated the idea of doing a profile of each of the workers within the Divisions of Celestial Stays, Lan had believed that it would be just a general, day-in-a-life piece.

That Kyra would want to know all the minutiae which she crammed in day after day.

And Lan felt as if she'd been naïve to allow herself to believe that.

Why *had* she allowed herself to believe that?

What Kyra wanted—it turned out—was nothing short of a blow-by-blow, potted account of Lan's life thus far. And, for some reason—she put it down to Kyra's wide-eyed, overly innocent, girlish act—Lan gave it to her.

There was something about Kyra which, in and of itself, seemed so completely inoffensive that there *seemed* to be no issue at all with opening up to her. Telling her *all* your secrets.

And, even as Lan allowed that whole strand of thought to flow through her brain, she realised just how idiotic she was being. She was doing nothing short of opening the door to a whole host of trouble. Hadn't she come to the Moon for a reason?

Hadn't she run away from *home* for a reason?

She had always wanted to hide just who she was . . . just what she had done . . .

And now, with Kyra beaming a mouthful of pearly white teeth at her, Lan realised that all the work she had put in would be for nothing.

Lan only realised how thoroughly she was under Kyra's power when it was Kyra who glanced up from her screen and declared that the session had finished for the day.

When Lan consulted the Link, sure enough, she saw that she only had fifteen minutes remaining on her shift. Back when they'd started off with these sessions, Lan had briefly wondered just what Duval would make of her spending her day spilling her guts about her not-so-sordid past instead of going through with her duties; but Kyra had quickly assuaged this fear—even before Lan had so much as put it into words—by declaring that this *was* a task which Frau Köhler herself had given her stamp of approval.

Lan couldn't fail but see her logic.

Unless Kyra was lying, of course.

But what was Lan going to do?

Was she going to initiate a private communication with Frau Köhler herself?

. . . Not likely.

With a smile—that same *girlish* smile—Kyra bid Lan goodbye, and Lan made her way back down through the Archive. When she got to the lobby, she was surprised to find that Patrick was there. He stood at the desk, speaking with Miguel.

As Lan descended the stairs, she caught Patrick's eye.

And she saw *something* there . . . *something* which she didn't quite understand.

Lan consciously told herself to smile. She thought about the times when she had been told to 'smile more' or to 'be friendlier' by various acquaintances.

This was perhaps the first time when the smile didn't feel forced.

It felt like the natural thing to do.

She and Patrick hadn't spoken since the night in the Infirmary.

She had wondered if it had something to do with timidity; with the fact that their relationship had moved on so quickly. She supposed that they both needed something of a timeout.

At least that was how *she'd* seen it . . .

For the first time, looking at Patrick now, seeing him glance back at her as if she was a stranger, she doubted herself. Perhaps she had been wrong. Maybe she'd read the signs all wrong. Had that kiss in the Crescent Gardens all been a ruse . . . a means for Patrick to work his way up to that unforgettable night in the Infirmary?

And was that all Patrick planned on it being: A *night*?

Now that she really thought about it, standing pinned by Miguel and Patrick's gaze, it all seemed to make sense. That she had just been a fool.

An *idiot*.

But she had to press on her public face.

She needed to remain calm; emotionless.

Thankfully, those qualities came easily to her.

Miguel was the first to speak. He smiled gently at her, clearly unsure about what it was exactly which'd passed between them, but obviously sensing *something* . . . then again, judging by the gossip which reached Lan's own ears, she knew that the Celestial Stays Dome wasn't exactly renowned for its sense of discretion.

"I was just telling him," Miguel said, "that you'd be down soon."

Lan turned her gaze onto Patrick.

So he *had* come here to find her.

For some reason this raised her spirits.

It condemned the crushing, nauseous feeling in her gut.

Patrick attempted a smile, but it reached no further than the corner of his mouth. "He says that you've been with Kyra."

Lan spun her gaze onto Miguel.

He looked back at her, innocently.

Of course he didn't have a clue what was going on.

How *could he* realise?

How could he know that Lan had already had a series of Very Serious Chats about the 'dangers' of Kyra?

All the same, Lan felt a flash of anger pass through her.

It would've been so easy for him to just say nothing at all; to stick to the bare essentials, that Lan, indeed, was currently posted to the Archive. He needn't have said anything at all about her being accompanied by Kyra.

Lan studied Patrick's expression. She didn't detect a change; at least no change from the stern expression he had apparently arrived to the Archive with.

She decided that the emphasis of the scenario was on her. She did her best to clear her voice, to keep her tone of voice firm and even; just like the image of the unyielding, deeply serious security guard she tried so hard to present. "What'd you want?" she asked, realising that in her directness she sounded quite rude.

Patrick blinked a couple of times, absorbing the effect of her words. "I . . . just thought that we . . . you know"—he flipped a glance in Miguel's direction, as if he was confirming that Lan was being unreasonable; this annoyed Lan no end—"we should have a chat?"

"A 'chat' ?" Lan replied, arching an eyebrow without thinking a thing about it.

As the silence draped down across them, she heard footsteps.

When she turned her head, she saw that it was Kyra.

That Kyra was leaving the Archive behind.

As if she wasn't tiptoeing her way through a bombsite, Kyra made her way out through the lobby and to the landing strip outside. It was only when Lan turned her attention onto Patrick

that she realised he—and Miguel—had been following her depar-
ture with intense scrutiny.

She wondered just how much Patrick had confided in Miguel.

Miguel, like everyone else under the Celestial Stays Dome,
knew just how untrustworthy Kyra was . . . how she was a viper in
the grass, ready to poison anyone to death so that she might have
some scrap to throw to her beloved Earthside media outlets.

Surely others would understand that Kyra had Frau Köhler's
backing?

Surely it wasn't such a big leap to make the connection that
Kyra's continued time on the Moon could only have been possible
with Frau Köhler's direct involvement?

. . . But, then again, Lan hadn't seen it herself; not before Kyra
had pointed it out to her.

Gradually, the PEAR which bore Kyra—to whatever her desti-
nation happened to be—rose up into the air, and it drifted off
across the Celestial Stays resort.

This sight seemed to act as the catalyst for the breaking of the
silence.

Patrick turned on Lan, then said, "Maybe we should just forget
about it, eh?"

And from the nonchalant expression he wore, and how he
shrugged a single shoulder, Lan was halfway to believing that he
really meant what he said. And she was all the way to believing
when he turned his back on her, and stalked his way out of the
Archive lobby, headed for the landing strip so that he might go and
catch his own PEAR.

Lan stood her ground for several seconds, feeling her heart
beating against the tender underside of her throat. And then she
threw off the inaction.

Under Miguel's watchful gaze, she stormed on after Patrick;

believing that she felt every inch as angry as Patrick himself. He wasn't the only one who felt thoroughly put out by whatever it was that had passed between them.

When she got outside, and she saw Patrick stepping into the PEAR which'd just set down on the landing strip, she broke into a run. She paid no attention to the gnawing—*numbing*—pain as it wracked her ribcage. When she got back to the Basements she could throw back a handful of pills . . . they'd fix her pain.

She caught Patrick by his arm—just as he made to draw it inside—before the PEAR's visor groaned shut. Somewhere from within the PEAR, a synthesised voice announced there was an obstruction, and that it should—*please*—be cleared as soon as possible.

Lan, of course, paid it no mind.

"What's the matter?" she said, her voice biting; icier still than it had been back in the Archive. "What's *got* into you?"

Patrick fixed her with a glare. She wondered if he would attempt to throw off her hold.

Ordinarily, she wouldn't have believed he would have a chance of beating her in a battle of strength, but with her cracked rib she had to admit that he'd probably never have a better opportunity. The key would be to *deny* him the opportunity in the first place.

Patrick said nothing.

His chest and shoulders rose and fell evenly with his breathing.

He parted his lips as if to speak, then, apparently giving up, he shook his head, and turned his face away from hers.

"Tell me," Lan said. "*Tell* me what's wrong."

She thought about her past self; how she might've dealt with a situation like this back down on Earth. There was no question. She would've simply walked away.

Just walked away.

"Is it Kyra?" Lan asked. "Is it because you're afraid I'll betray Gofreddo to her?"

Patrick met her eye. He held still for the longest time. Then shook his head.

"Then *what*?" she said, widening her eyes; already wondering if she hadn't given away too much to Patrick . . . if she hadn't just betrayed the trust—or whatever it'd been—which Alicia had invested in her.

Patrick finally relaxed his posture. Then he nodded to the PEAR; to the twin seats within. "Shall we go for a ride?" he asked. "I've had a tough day."

Although Lan would've liked nothing more than to fight harder; than to do her very best to win the argument, to absolve herself of blame, she decided to let the matter drop.

And she clambered into the PEAR alongside Patrick.

26

TIME AWAY

*T*he *Shuttle* trundled over the lunar plains at cruising velocity.

Lan sat in silence in the co-pilot's seat beside Patrick.

Being in this position—sat beside the pilot—took her back to her childhood; particularly to her days in the Cadets when she'd gone along on flights with instructors; and the many times her parents had taken her out flying.

She recalled the times she'd gone out with her parents as some of her happiest childhood memories; mostly because she recalled —*at least in her mind's eye*—that her parents were constantly smiling . . . there seemed no greater thrill for them than taking to the air.

Lan supposed that she'd believed for the longest time that she shared the same passion for aviation, although, in reality, it seemed that she had merely been absorbing her parents' enthusiasm. Sucking up their passion second-hand and believing it to be her own.

Sitting here in the Shuttle cockpit—beside Patrick—she could honestly say that she had no interest whatsoever in taking the controls off him.

She had none of that curiosity which'd surrounded machines during her childhood.

She watched the lunar plains drift by beneath them.

Several times she had glanced to Patrick, hoping to prompt him into spilling just what was on his mind. On more than a few occasions, she had had to actively restrain herself from questioning him directly . . . from *bleeding* the problem out of him.

She needed to exercise patience.

Finally, when they'd got about ten minutes out of the Dome, Patrick did open up.

He told her about Gofreddo Zito, and how he had been neglecting what Patrick termed 'maintenance' duties around the Shuttle Hangar. Although it sounded like a dull matter to Lan, she could tell, from Patrick's tone of voice, and the dramatic action he'd taken—filing a report with Supervisor Mackenzie Angliss— that it was *far* from being 'dull'.

Patrick had filed the report days earlier but it was only today that Mackenzie Angliss had taken decisive action. She had sent along a group of Security Division members to relieve Gofreddo of his current role of Shuttle pilot.

With tears beginning to sparkle in his eyes, Patrick relayed the moment when the members of Security, led by Supervisor Duval— Lan's boss—had arrived to take Gofreddo away from the Shuttle Hangar. Patrick explained how Gofreddo had met his eye, and how he had given him the purest look of hurt—of *pain*—that Patrick had had the misfortune to receive.

When Patrick was through with his detailing of events, he explained that he had lost his best friend that day; he was *sure* of it.

They passed over the Lunar One Monument—one of the tent poles of the standard tour which was offered to the Celestial Stays clientele.

Lan peered down on the protective bubble which covered the Lunar One Monument.

When she snuck a sidelong glance at Patrick, she saw that he, too, was staring down at the Monument; that he was considering it . . . perhaps the thought that Gofreddo Zito's grandparents were buried beneath it brought him back to thinking of his best friend.

And how he had betrayed him.

Lan expected the seemingly aimless voyage over the lunar plains to come to a sudden halt, but it didn't seem like Patrick was ready to turn around and go back home.

Not yet.

He flew them on up to the North Pole, then around a few times, turning circles.

When Lan managed to catch his eye, she saw that he was smiling lightly, as if he was allowing his mind to escape into this childlike game . . . the spaceship pilot's equivalent of standing with arms stretched out and spinning round on the spot in ever-tightening circles.

After several dozen rotations and Lan—*at least*—beginning to feel a touch dizzy, Patrick steered them back off across the lunar plains. Although Lan was far from being an expert on lunar navigation, she had been out in Shuttles enough times to know that they were passing over familiar terrain. That they were indeed on their way back home.

Lan wondered if she would go and visit the gym; but just the thought of doing so sent a pang of pain jangling through her ribcage. If the gym was off the menu for the time being then just how was *she* supposed to unwind? And with that realisation certain—*wicked*—thoughts snuck into her brain. She turned to Patrick. "Do you mind if we set down somewhere around here?"

"Hmm?" Patrick replied, apparently distracted by the terrain opening out ahead of them; of guiding the Shuttle along the pathway he must've had so deeply engrained into his mind.

When he looked back at her, she realised that she must've been smiling.

Because he smiled at *her*.

"Okey doke," Patrick said, and then eased the Shuttle down toward the lunar surface.

When he brought the Shuttle in to land, Lan felt her stomach rise briefly. It was a sudden sense of fear—the knowledge that they were out here, totally alone.

There being no strip to set down upon, Patrick activated the rough terrain landing gear.

She watched as frown lines sketched his forehead, as he tensed his muscles, seemingly vexing every nerve in his body; channelling all the concentration he possessed into the task of bringing them down with a safe landing.

Lan could bring to mind countless pilots back on Earth who had put on that same face of extreme concentration. She wondered what might go through the mind of a pilot to know that every occupant of their ship was depending on their skill; on their attention to detail . . . on their *patience*.

Finally, Patrick brought the Shuttle to a standstill.

She noticed how he straightened his back, and how the tension seemed to leave his shoulders as he clicked off the propulsion systems.

They wouldn't need them for the time being.

Acting on animal urge, Lan snapped free of her shoulder restraints, and leaped at Patrick.

She probably would've knocked him clean from his chair if it hadn't been for Patrick's own restraints. And, as it was, she was better able to get a solid grip on him . . . to wrap her legs about his hardened flanks. To seize him in her vice-like hold.

She heard the gasp escape his lips.

Felt his warm breath against her throat.

And she thrust her tongue hard into his mouth.

Apparently stunned at this turn of events, Patrick took more than a few heartbeats to respond. But, when he did, it was with hunger . . . a hunger which revealed just how badly he had needed her; how badly he had been *waiting* for her.

She worked quickly at his overalls, freeing him from the grey-white flight suit; soon getting him down to his underwear while remaining sitting in his lap.

Patrick pulled back a moment, panting. "Seems like I'm a little ahead."

Lan smirked then reached up for the zipper of her own overalls.

She eyed him closely as she brought it down slowly, as she listened to the gentle sound of the unzipping. As she unzipped a little more each time, she observed his eyes becoming wider and wider. She liked to believe that it was his hunger becoming deeper and *deeper*.

Now the two of them were down to their underwear—and equality, apparently, had been established—Lan turned her attention to the cockpit around them.

"There's nothing here we're going to break, is there?"

Patrick reached up his hand to point. "Well, there's the—"

But Lan didn't give him the chance to finish, pressing her mouth hard up against Patrick's.

She felt his soft lips against hers, and she could taste his *sweet* taste within.

She fumbled at the waistband of his flight overalls.

He didn't resist her.

And soon he was naked.

Naked *and* at the controls of the Shuttle.

Knowing that she couldn't afford to let her advantage slide, she bent over him, took him in her mouth. She felt him grow harder there. And she felt a *groan* pass through his body in a series of vibrations. She felt his pulse against her tongue, and then, when she felt his pulse match her own, she drew back—*pinned* him with her stare.

She looked into his hazel eyes.

Like a pair of pure amber drops.

She wondered if she might be able to read her fortune in those disparate patterns and textures.

She wondered if she might be able to lose herself for eternity.

Patrick finally regained his strength—apparently shoving away his worries surrounding the day. He took hold of her; determined to take charge of the encounter from here on out.

And Lan took it as another piece of evidence of her growing inner strength that she allowed him that privilege. That she surrendered herself to him . . . losing herself totally.

Utterly.

INCOMING TRANSMISSION

*J*ié Niu was sat at her desk, working out what she was going to do with the overwhelming applications which filled the inbox of her Link when another, more urgent message arrived.

As it was marked *URGENT* the message pushed itself to the top of the pile.

Since these *URGENT* messages occurred dozens of times daily, Jié only treated the message with a degree of interest.

However, by the time she had read the first three words of the attached file, she was hooked.

And the rest of her work was forgotten.

It was an article, one which had been published in an English-language media outlet. When she rushed up to the timestamp at the top of the attachment, she saw that it had been in circulation for the best part of twenty-four hours. Although the government had comprehensive filters and search algorithms which covered all global media outlets, it tended to take its time when it came to poring through material in English . . . it had something to do with translation.

Sometimes Jié wondered if it wouldn't have been a more efficient system to put some fluent English-speaker to work on the task.

Then again, twenty-four hours was impossibly faster than she might've imagined intelligence reaching her from source back when she had commenced her career.

Jié picked her way through the original English article, faltering whenever she reached a particularly important sentence and going back to give it a second read; second guessing herself as to whether or not she had truly appreciated the meaning.

But, when she got to the end, she had no lingering doubt over just what the article meant.

What it meant for her daughter's safety.

The article took the form of a profile—what professed to be the first in a series covering the various 'Divisions'; the organisational structure; of the Celestial Stays operation . . . the one of which Lan —Jié's daughter—was a part.

As Jié well knew, her daughter had signed on for a contract to work in the Security Division. However, not only did Lan go into detail about her day-to-day routine, along with all its—*surprisingly military*—mundanity, but she also explored, with teasing scraps, areas of her past. And, especially, in one notable paragraph, her relationship with her parents.

Or, put more accurately, her *non*-relationship with her parents.

How her parents were so ashamed of their daughter that they had gone to the trouble of publically *faking* her death.

When Jié had got through with reading the article on her Link, she felt her heart pulsing hard and low. Her stomach was crunching in on itself.

She wondered what it might mean. Of course she *knew* what it surely meant.

The kidnappers—the ones who had sent Jié and her husband the threat—would have seen this media communication. They would know Lan was alive. And on the Moon.

Jié laid her elbows down on her desk, and, slowly, brought her hands up to her temples. She massaged the indentations in her skull, hoping to at least soothe her aching brain to some degree.

But she knew it would do no good.

She was close to losing her mind.

Despite the many emotions which threatened to burst free of her—to cloud the prized logical-thinking which'd brought her so far along her career path—Jié managed to control herself.

She took deep breaths.

And she wondered just what the implications would *exactly* be.

Did the kidnappers have the capacity—the *resources*—to reach Lan up on the Moon?

Might they pay for one of their members to go up there, and to remove Lan by force?

Frustratingly, Jié knew that she couldn't rule it out.

All the intelligence she had so far received suggested that the group was a professional outfit. And that they'd stop at nothing to blackmail the ROCAF . . . let alone Jié and Yŏng.

It was then that Jié glanced up from her desk.

Her heart pounded in her eardrums.

She ran back over the thought which'd just crossed her mind.

It couldn't work, could it?

What were the wider implications . . . was there a limit to what she would do for her daughter?

As Jié decided that there was no other option—that there could be no other way—she pressed her finger into her earpiece and sent off the command through her neural implant.

DAYS OF INTERFACE

*I*f someone had told Lan—even so much as two weeks ago —that she, *Lan Niu,* would have a skip in her step, the constant image of a *man* in her mind, she would've thought them crazy.

Or, most likely, she would've just thought it was a joke at her expense.

Yes, she supposed there was a certain attraction to making stern, po-faced Lan Niu the butt of whatever joke happened to be in the offing that particular day.

Lan positively danced her way through the Security HQ locker rooms, stashing her blaster pistol away until her next shift; tearing off her jet-black, dour Security overalls and putting on, instead, a smoky-grey little cocktail dress.

She was meeting Patrick in about half an hour, when he got off his own shift, and they were planning an expedition to the Lunar Caverns. Although Lan had been in and out of the Lunar Caverns in her time, it had always been while she was on duty; tracking this or that lost person . . . the most notable time had been with Alex Barn, when Louise Williams had heroically faced off with him. Lan had been the one to show her the way—the secret tunnel which ran from the Stellar Tide Casino to the Caverns themselves.

As Lan ventured forth from Security HQ, she noticed right away that Louise Williams and Alicia Brennan were alighting a nearby PEAR. The two of them had their gaze fixed on her, and Lan couldn't help but think that they'd been lying in wait.

Indeed, Lan hardly got herself five steps from the Security HQ doorway before Alicia and Louise were upon her; before the two of them were up in her face.

Lan did her best to play down any trace of aggression they might be picking up off her. Though, to tell the truth, she wasn't quite sure how she might come across as threatening in a cocktail dress this short . . . All the same, she held her hands down at her sides.

"We need to talk," Alicia said, without so much as an introduction, and, this time at least, no trace of the easy, friendly smile which seemed to be permanently pressed onto her lips.

Before Lan could respond, Louise had looped her arm through one elbow, before Alicia had looped her arm through Lan's other elbow.

They frogmarched her to the PEAR they'd arrived in, and waited for her to get inside.

Deciding that neither of them were likely to harm her—*she was certain that she could break either of their arms in a matter of seconds*—she allowed them to have their way.

Together, the visor still coming down on the PEAR, they lifted up into the air and began to drift across the Celestial Stays resort.

Neither Alicia or Louise spoke, and Lan wasn't exactly going to be the one to break the silence. She wanted to know what sort of danger she was in before she gave anything away.

Just what she might be able to give away beat Lan momentarily . . .

While she was undoubtedly a private person—except when it came to Patrick—Lan didn't consider herself to have any Deep Dark Secrets. Then again, as she'd always learned from her parents —*mostly from her mother*—what seemed to be insignificant or trivial to one person might prove to be immeasurably valuable to another. Was that the reason why she'd always been so introverted? Why she'd always been so afraid about giving something *away*?

The PEAR swept downward, eventually coming to rest on the landing strip outside the Lunar Grand. Lan's mind boggled as to why they'd come *here* of all places.

And neither Louise or Alicia seemed interested in explaining.

The PEAR's visor swished back and—again under Louise and Alicia's control—Lan found herself being escorted along. Together, they ventured forth into the lobby of the Lunar Grand.

They'd risen up half the building before Lan had even the slightest inkling of what was going on. She somehow got to thinking that it might have something to do with Gofreddo Zito . . . with what Patrick had revealed to her about Gofreddo . . . about how he had been turfed out of his Shuttle-pilot duty for negligence.

Surreptitiously, Lan slipped Alicia a sidelong glance, attempting to divine whether or not she might give something away. Surely if this had something to do with her lover then she would've been far more riled.

Lan looked up.

Mackenzie Angliss's office.

Although Lan had never been here herself, she had heard the stories.

What they said about gossiping beneath the Celestial Stays Dome was true.

Mackenzie Angliss's office—just as Lan had heard—had wall-to-wall windows and it looked out over the entirety of the Celestial Stays resort.

For several seconds, Land was rendered hypnotised by the skyline.

It was *quite* a view.

"Come on," Alicia said, her voice insistent; hinting that Lan might've been right in her assumption that this had something to do with Gofreddo.

She sensed *anger.*

Between them, Lan was hustled along to Mackenzie Angliss's office.

Mackenzie herself was standing with her finger stuffed into her inner-ear, delivering some message through her neural implant. She turned, looked out through the glass, and then summoned them into her office. Lan stood her ground, only realising after a few seconds that neither Louise or Alicia were urging her along.

"She wants to speak with you alone," Alicia said, her voice deadpan.

Those blueberry muffins Alicia had brought her in the Infirmary seemed an awfully long way away in the past now.

Lan glanced to Alicia, and then to Louise.

Then, seeing that Mackenzie was staring at her, Lan decided she had no other choice.

She would have to go inside.

"Shut the door, will you?"

Mackenzie's tone was sharp.

Although Mackenzie was a long way from what Lan believed was a *warm* individual, she was normally much more personable than she clearly was today.

Lan wondered what she'd done wrong.

Why the mood was so sombre.

And why Louise and Alicia—beyond the glass, soundproof walls of Mackenzie's office—continued to prowl like a pair of hyenas . . . as if they were afraid that Lan might break loose at a moment's notice and escape their clutches forever.

Lan decided that Mackenzie's demand was borne out of some sort of stress—or extreme *habit*—because the door, like every other door beneath the Celestial Stays Dome, had already swept closed of its own accord. Maybe Mackenzie's mind was fixed back on Earth.

Lan shifted her gaze away from Alicia and Louise, and back onto Mackenzie. "Am I in trouble?" she asked, feeling her voice break slightly.

She silently reprimanded herself.

She had given something away.

She'd given away her state of mind . . . her *anxiety*.

Mackenzie glanced over Lan's head, flurried her hand at Louise and Alicia.

After a brief pause, Louise and Alicia—*reluctantly*—retreated from Mackenzie's office.

They disappeared off around the corner.

Lan wasn't convinced that they would forget about her.

"I'm sorry about that," Mackenzie said, with a slight pout. "They were the only ones I could truly trust; the only ones I could *truly*, really, deep-in-my-heart trust."

"Oh-kay," Lan replied, stretching the first syllable.

Mackenzie again reached up to her inner earpiece, jabbed her finger in there, and issued some other silent order. She blinked rapidly several times, and Lan realised that, whatever the reason, Mackenzie felt as if she was under extreme pressure.

Why?

Again, Lan felt that she should step in here.

"Has this got something to do with Gofreddo Zito—with *Patrick?*"

The moment Patrick's name left her lips, Lan realised she had acted indiscreetly; failing to tack on his surname, to make him sound more like a professional acquaintance and less of a passionate fling. It *was* only a 'fling', wasn't it?

Mackenzie shook her head, making a few strands of red hair slip free of her ponytail. "No—although, I suppose your relationship with Patrick might have something to do with Alicia's *ire* . . ."

Lan thought to herself that first it had been Kyra, and now it was Patrick.

It didn't seem like she could possibly win.

Mackenzie continued, "No," she said, "it's something else. Something more serious."

Lan felt her chest tighten.

Her ribs ached.

What could be more serious than what Patrick had explained to her about Gofreddo?

From what Patrick had said, Gofreddo might've put everyone beneath the Celestial Stays Dome's lives in danger. And now Lan had done something worse?

Something *more* serious?

"This morning I received a message—*Earthside Comms.*"

Lan felt another pang of pain through her ribcage.

She bit down on her tongue to prevent herself from showing any external reaction.

"What did it say?" Lan replied, her voice cooler, more measured than she'd imagined it would be.

Mackenzie gave Lan a resilient smile, then she glanced out the window; out across the Celestial Stays resort. "That your life is in danger."

Strangely, Lan felt nothing to hear that statement come from Mackenzie's mouth.

She didn't know exactly what she'd expected, but it had been along those lines.

Why else all the gravity?

All the *seriousness*?

"Who says so?" Lan asked.

Mackenzie breathed in deeply, as if she was trying to enter some trance so that she could better concentrate on the matter at hand. "Your parents."

This time Lan was surprised.

"My *parents*?" And then, before she could control herself, she added, "The ones who had me *killed off* in the media?"

Only a second or so after she'd said it did Lan realise the implications of what she'd said; that she hadn't only put her own foot in it, but Kyra's too.

Mackenzie gave Lan a cool glance, and then nodded in reply.

It seemed that she had been aware of this development also.

Just another thing that Lan had to thank Kyra for.

"Listen, Niu," Mackenzie said, striking a no-nonsense tone now, "there's not much time. I've received orders that you're to be placed in a secure location until further notice."

This was all so surreal.

Lan cocked her head to one side.

"What's 'until further notice'?"

"When your parents get here."

This was by far the biggest shock Lan had experienced in a long time.

She wasn't sure how to handle it.

Of course, to hear that her parents had bothered to contact Mackenzie—to let her know that her life was in danger—had been a bolt from the blue, but to hear that they were . . . that they were . . . *actually coming*.

Lan turned her attention back to Mackenzie. "I don't understand," she said. "How can they . . . *afford* to take the trip?"

Mackenzie gave a shrug, but it wasn't out of indifference, it was out of genuine ignorance. "I don't know," she replied. "I only know what I've told you. If you want answers then I'd suggest you'd be better off speaking to them when they arrive here."

"When're they arriving?" Lan asked, her voice skipping slightly.

Mackenzie stuck her finger into her inner ear, looked into mid-air for a beat—that tell-tale sign of someone examining a screen in their mind's eye—then she shifted her attention back onto Lan. "They just left Earth . . . I'd imagine they'll be here in a day, maybe two."

Lan suddenly felt very faint.

And her ribcage throbbed hard.

She wondered if they'd allow her to go pick up some of her pain pills before she was placed in a 'secure location'.

SECURE LOCATION

*L*an wasn't all that sure what to make of the hiding place which Mackenzie Angliss picked out for her. It turned out to be a basement beneath the Orbital Café . . . what had been Alicia Brennan's pride and joy before her promotion to Supervisor of Catering.

If stuffing her beneath the floorboards was the idea of a cutting-edge solution for hiding a person, then Lan had to admit that she didn't much rate the collective Celestial Stays brainpower. Then again, she supposed that she should be pleased at how concerned they apparently were for her well-being.

Lan had been aware of how closely Louise and Alicia had guarded her; which was to say that they had hurried her out of the Lunar Grand, and into the PEAR waiting on the landing strip outside. Neither one of them had said anything to her, and Lan had felt distinctly uncomfortable to be sandwiched between them on the ride over to the Orbital Café.

Once they had delivered Lan to the basement of the Orbital Café, they had left her alone.

The basement wasn't without its charms.

There was a mattress on the floor—ostensibly for her to sleep on—and a few crates which contained various supplies.

Unfortunately, they didn't much deliver on the promise which the sweet smell lingering on the air offered; just the standard small sachets of powders which would keep Lan alive in the meantime.

Lan had resigned herself to the boredom which the basement seemed to serve up when she heard the sound of footsteps above her head. She turned to the door which led up the stairs, saw it creak open. She supposed that whoever was on the other side was taking special care not to cause a fuss above ground. To be *subtle* about their movements.

When she focussed on who it was coming through the doorway, she realised that it was Patrick.

Her heart did a little flip.

And her mind felt a quick rush.

She rose up off the floor. And she trod toward him.

Before he could so much as utter a word, she threw her arms about him. She squeezed his body to her own, and felt his warmth. Her whole body seized tight. And she felt his muscles rigid. He seemed larger down here, in the low light of the basement. When she breathed in, she caught the sweet baking smell from upstairs clinging to his overalls.

"I came as soon as I could," he said. "When I heard what'd happened."

Lan peeled herself away from him. "You mean that Mackenzie told you where I was?"

Patrick shrugged his shoulders, then grinned. "Apparently— how else would I have got here?"

"Maybe Louise or Alicia told you."

"Not likely; neither of them are speaking to me because of what I did to Gofreddo."

Lan allowed Patrick's words to drift away into the stilted basement air before replying. "You did what you had to do—you weren't to blame . . . *Gofreddo* was the one to blame."

Patrick remained very still for the longest time, and then he shook his head as if to dismiss this. "I could've spoken to him before . . . I had enough chances . . . if I hadn't been a coward then I would've done just that—it would've softened the blow; it wouldn't have made it such a backstabbing manoeuvre."

Seeing Patrick's current state of mind, Lan decided not to say anything at all.

When Patrick had apparently got past his current wonderings directed at Gofreddo—his best friend—he looked at Lan with a freshly sharp gaze. "What about you?" he said, widening his eyes. "What's *this* all about? Why all the secrecy?"

Lan felt as if something invisible was weighing down her shoulders. "I don't know—Mackenzie . . . she said . . ." But Lan realised that she couldn't get out another word.

Was she crying?

Could she feel tears forming in the corners of her eyes?

Her whole body felt rigid, as she got whenever she attempted to push down her feelings.

Whenever she tried to keep herself from those visceral, *untidy* reactions.

"It's okay," Patrick said.

She looked up, looked to his eyes.

"You don't need to push it down . . . you don't need to be anyone else but yourself with me."

Her heart beat harder.

It was like all this was happening in slow motion.

As if they were here—*together*—and yet the whole world was falling down around them.

It was then that she felt Patrick reach out and stroke her cheek. His skin was warm, and it banished the chill which'd set into her blood almost immediately. Her whole body quivered.

"Let's put you to bed," he said, and, taking her by the wrist— firmly but gently—he led her over to the mattress lying on the floor.

He took great care to place her down on the mattress and then to lower himself beside her. His chest rose and fell with a calm rhythm against his overalls.

Lan could feel her own breathing getting out of control.

She had to struggle for every breath.

Air never seemed enough.

Again, Patrick seemed to anticipate this. He reached out and stroked her cheek.

All of a sudden, he made any negative emotion in her body disappear . . . he simply made it disintegrate into nothing. It was only now—only now that she was lying on her back, beside him— that she realised she had waited for someone like this for her entire life.

That she had *wished* for someone like this her entire life.

Even in her lowest moments—even in her most *resilient* moments of loneliness; when she had wished to be with no one but herself.

Patrick had been the one she'd waited for.

She saw that now.

Understood that now.

As he slowly undressed her, unzipping her overalls, she felt her heartbeat lowering to a steady *thum*. Her whole mind phased in, and out. She wondered if she might faint from happiness . . . and that seemed so ridiculous. Here she was—*stashed away; apparently in danger*—and she was acknowledging that she was truly *happy*.

But she was.

As Patrick lowered himself down onto her, as she felt his lips come close to hers, she heard the words which he whispered. And she wondered if she might hear them over and over again —*repeated*—until the day she died.

"I love you."

30

REMOVAL

*P*atrick *stirred from his sleep,* hearing the footsteps overhead.

It was dark down here, in the basement. One of them had turned out the small light which provided the only means of illumination.

He reached about himself, feeling the mattress, and then Lan, lying beside him.

Working quickly, Patrick grabbed his overalls, and slipped himself within.

There was a knock followed by a muttered word.

Patrick rose and zipped up just as the door opened.

"Just a minute!" he called out.

There seemed to be a pause on the other side of the door.

He took his opportunity to carefully wake Lan, and to help her into her own overalls.

With the two of them blinking from the harsh light leaking into the basement, Patrick used his forearm to shield his eyes. They stumbled their way together to the doorway.

Patrick soon found himself nose to nose with Mackenzie Angliss.

Despite everything—despite this apparently *fraught* situation—Mackenzie managed to raise a smile to him. "I see you managed to find one another." She smirked when she turned her attention onto Lan. "I hope you were able to get *some* rest."

When Patrick looked to Lan, he saw that she was blushing.

He switched back to Mackenzie. "What's happening now?" he asked. "Where're we *going?*"

When Mackenzie replied, however, she addressed Lan. "Your parents arrived about an hour or so ago. They're staying in the Blue Moon Suite, at the Lunar Grand."

Patrick observed Lan, wondering how she might react to this news.

There was so much he still didn't know about Lan; about her family, about her upbringing. But he was determined to find out all he could . . . he would just have to be patient; there was no way that he would be able to figure out everything all at once.

"This way," Mackenzie said, gesturing off into the Orbital Café.

As they left the Orbital Café basement behind, Patrick couldn't help but shift a final glance back over his shoulder, to what'd been their love nest for the evening. Although he only had the faintest idea of what was going on—but with the knowledge that Lan might well be in danger—he felt somewhat ashamed to have enjoyed the previous night.

But, then again, snatching a glance at Lan, and seeing her beam a wide smile back at him, he decided that he wasn't the only one who enjoyed the previous night.

When they reached the door of the Orbital Café, Mackenzie

stopped Patrick and Lan, telling them to wait where they were. Mackenzie left through the doorway—venturing outside—leaving Lan and Patrick alone for a long while.

Lan turned into Patrick, a slight smile still lining her lips.

On impulse, Patrick leaned into her, pressing his mouth up against hers.

They held their pose for a long while, Lan massaging his lower lip with her tongue.

He felt warmth down in the pit of his stomach, and his whole body became rigid.

Ready.

There was a cough nearby.

Both of them turned.

Mackenzie stood in the doorway, arching an eyebrow. "When you're ready, Lan, your parents are waiting for you."

Although it was subtle—the slightest of gestures which was present one second and gone the next—Patrick caught the wince which passed over Lan's features. She tried to cover it up with a smile, but it was too late.

"What's wrong?" Patrick said, looking from Lan to Mackenzie. "Why can't I come?"

Mackenzie gave a rough sigh; the type of sigh which—Patrick imagined—she reserved for new arrivals who couldn't seem to grasp the fundamentals of life beneath the Dome.

Some days, Patrick would admit, he wondered if he'd fully grasped the fundamentals of the Dome himself . . .

"You've got your duties to attend to," Mackenzie replied.

When Patrick checked the Link, sure enough, he had duties for that day.

In fact, he needed to be on duty within the next half an hour.

His heart quickened as he thought about catching a quick

shower before heading out across the lunar plains. One thing was for certain, now that he had reduced the Shuttle pilot roster, he had plenty of work to attend to. That had been another disadvantage of grassing up his best friend.

He glanced back at Lan, his mouth slightly parted.

Before he could raise his voice, Mackenzie beat him to the punch.

"It's okay," she said, with a vague smile. "We'll take good care of her."

Patrick considered this another moment, still undecided.

Mackenzie, apparently an expert in reading people, continued, "If we thought she was in any sort of *serious* danger do you really think we would've let you come see her last night?"

Patrick thought on this.

He wasn't really sure *what* to think.

He felt Lan's touch against his hand.

He glanced down.

Saw how she entangled her fingers about his own.

And *squeezed*.

"Go on," Lan said, "it'll be okay." She smiled widely. "I *promise*."

Patrick hung back another few seconds, unsure what he should do.

In the end, Mackenzie was the one who broke the standoff, grabbing hold of Lan's other—*unoccupied*—hand, and dragging her out through the doorway of the Orbital Café.

Patrick stood stunned on the doorstep, distantly aware of the delightful, sweet smells all around him. And he couldn't help wondering—despite the situation; despite the *peril* which Lan might currently find herself in—if Alicia might be by shortly to rustle something up in the kitchen.

REPROCESSED MEMORIES

ot in all of her gym sessions in all her life had Lan felt her heart pounding away against her ribs as it pounded away right now. Blood pumped to her head. Her palms felt clammy. All at once, she felt somehow underdressed to be wearing her standard, black Security Division overalls.

She wondered what her parents might make of her.

Who *knew* what her parents would make of her?

There was only one way to be sure.

And that was by walking through the doorway and into the Blue Moon Suite.

Lan had left Mackenzie behind at the lift doors. Mackenzie had at least trusted Lan to make it to the Blue Moon Suite without getting herself into trouble. After the way she'd been treated in the past twenty-four hours, Lan supposed that she should've felt proud on some level about that.

But any potential sense of pride was replaced by pure anxiety.

Fifteen years . . . had it really been that long?

It had to be close, at least.

If Lan had had any nerve at all then she might've been able to manage a smile at the craziness of this whole situation. Who would've thought that—after the best part of fifteen years—she would be reunited with her parents, on the *Moon*?

With her heart in her throat, Lan reached out for the door and knocked.

The room fell upon Lan like a sea.

So many different shades of blue.

She took in the furnishings; the sofas, the chairs, and the picture frames . . . all of them the royal-blue of Celestial Stays.

The wallpaper was powder-blue.

Perhaps—if circumstances had been different—it would've had a calming effect on her.

As she shuffled tentatively forward, she noted the faintly blue carpet beneath her feet, which reminded her of fine lunar dust.

The suite had a window which looked out over the lunar plains themselves.

From here, Lan could get a good view of the Shuttle Hangar.

Even now—even at this; the *most fraught* of moments—she found her thoughts drifting away from her; settling onto Patrick.

God . . . she hadn't thought of *that*.

What might her parents think of *Patrick*?

It was a wonder that she noticed her parents at all; so still were the two of them sitting in the armchairs. For several moments, Lan took them to be the proverbial statues.

The two of them were staring into mid-air.

Neither of them had turned to look at Lan as she had entered.

And neither one of them made a move to look at her now.

Her heart clenched tightly.

And a hot burst of blood ran about her veins.

She took in their appearances. It was strange that their faces were exactly how Lan remembered them to be; only that her mother—*Jiě's*—hair had turned white. She had decided against dying it black like many other women of her age did.

Lan was glad that she hadn't dyed her hair; it gave her a distinctive look.

A *wise* look.

Her father—*Yǒng*—struck a decidedly different pose.

Lan couldn't help but settle on the idea that he had shrunk. That the wrinkles now hung slack from his throat; that his cheekbones were no longer pristine, and carved, as they had once been. He had lost weight, of that Lan was certain. Although her father had never been a large man, he had always had a tight collection of muscles. He had always looked fit; *trim*—like Lan herself in many ways.

Now, though, the muscle was gone. And there hadn't come any fat to replace it.

No merry, jiggling 'beer-belly'—as she had often heard Anglo-Saxon colleagues describe it. And neither had his hair thinned noticeably. But—like her mother's—his hair *had* turned grey.

Again—like her mother—it lent him a *distinguished* appearance.

A *grand* appearance.

The two of them wore the distinctive burgundy overalls of Celestial Stays guests, though how they could be 'officially' guests still escaped Lan. Although the two of them had had wildly successful careers in the ROCAF, neither could have possibly gathered together the resources required for so much as a short stay beneath the Dome. But, then again, since she hadn't seen them in so long, was it so difficult to imagine that they might've done something else?

That they might've accumulated the capital through some other means?

Might *this* be the reason why Lan had come into danger . . . the unwitting daughter of a pair of billionaires? Made a target by kidnappers looking for a cash payoff?

"Mum?" Lan said, trying out her voice. *"Dad?"*

Her parents—as if her voice was a tonic which brought them around from a daze—turned their attention onto her. Well, that was something. At least they could *hear* her.

And hopefully now they could *see* her.

"I . . . uh . . ." Lan began, but couldn't continue.

She thought of Mackenzie Angliss, standing not too far from the room. She wondered if she might be standing close by the door, and—if she was—whether or not she spoke Shanghainese with any degree of fluency. Even if she spoke some Mandarin— like several others did on Earth—she would struggle greatly to understand more than the broadest strokes of the Shanghainese she spoke with her parents.

No, Lan could be fairly confident that she wouldn't be over-heard here.

Even though it was her mother tongue, it felt strange—*unwieldy almost*—for her to be speaking it out loud. She had spent so much of the past decade and a half speaking English that she felt dim-witted. *Slow.*

"It has been . . . uhm"—Lan took a moment to think of the appropriate idiom—"*a long while . . .*"

Her parents remained so still that Lan doubted whether they were real.

If they were in fact here.

If this was—*really*—happening.

Her heartbeat had slowed now.

No longer did she feel the tap of her pulse at the underside of her throat.

And yet, she didn't feel any better.

Any less apprehensive.

At last, it was her mother who spoke.

Still sitting, her voice just about rose above a whisper.

"Yes," she replied. "It *has* been a long while."

Lan was surprised at the subdued atmosphere. Although what she might've expected from her parents—who had never been anything other than understated, subdued, throughout her childhood—she couldn't rightly say. Perhaps she expected *some* show of emotion.

Just the glistening of a tear in the corner of an eye.

Or the vaguest of smiles.

Even a wide-eyed examination.

They didn't even seem *interested* in her.

And it was then that Lan decided she *must* be dead.

At least in *their* minds.

Her mother explained how—ever since Lan had left the childhood home—they had kept watch on her. She even explained that the ROCAF—the *government*—had footed a large amount of the bill to do so. That they were afraid what kinds of secrets Lan might be willing to reveal to 'state enemies'. As her mother explained Lan couldn't help wondering why the government—if they were truly so concerned about her leaking information—

hadn't simply locked her up when she'd attempted to leave the country behind.

Or why they hadn't had her surreptitiously killed by some international assassin.

The upshot of the whole ordeal was that her parents had kept a very close eye over seemingly every last one of her activities throughout the past decade or so. They knew about her every movement—*from country to country*—and they knew about her every last *job* . . .

That she had decided to take on the mantle of a security guard.

When Lan scanned her mother's tone, searching for any sign of disapproval, she was surprised to find there seemed to be none. It seemed as if her mother simply relayed the facts.

The cold, hard facts.

Or perhaps it was because Lan hadn't spoken her first language for so long that she was missing the subtleties of mood which it conveyed.

She hardly felt herself any longer. And as to whether she had ever been the person her parents had *hoped* she'd become, that ship had sailed long ago.

Lan was bursting with questions once her mother had coolly re-laid just how closely they'd kept a watch on her through the previous years. But she knew better—even the best part of two decades later—than to interrupt her mother.

Insubordination, for either her mother, or father, was preferable only to *treason*.

When Lan did get her chance to speak up, she took full advantage.

Although she'd been standing off to the side of the others for the longest time, she now took several steps toward her parents. She noticed how the two of them fixed her with an equally level

—*unmovable*—gaze. She wondered if a trip to the Moon didn't manage to shift them of their natural-born stoicism if anything in the universe *would* do so.

"If what you are telling me is true," Lan said, her arms feeling awkward as she allowed them to dangle down at her sides. "If you knew exactly where I was all this time—if you knew my *precise* location—then why did you never try to get in touch with me? Why did you never *contact* me?"

Her parents remained very still.

This time it was her father who spoke up.

"We wanted you to make your own decisions." He glanced to Lan's mother, as if they might be capable of telepathically sending signals from one to the other. He shifted his attention back to Lan. "You always knew that you could come home; that we would always be waiting." Here a slight smile crept onto his lips. "That you could *return*."

Lan studied his voice again, wondering if there was some other message which she just wasn't able to pick up on. It would be just like her to miss something obvious in the subtext of her own father's voice; she who had spent so much of her life *alone* . . . attempting to wriggle free of the company of others.

"We did not wish to force you," Lan's mother put in. "We wanted to respect your own life decisions. We wanted you to make up your mind for yourself."

Now it was Lan's turn to feel ashamed.

Why hadn't she ever got in touch with them?

Had she *genuinely* believed that her parents no longer cared about her?

That they had simply *forgotten* her?

As if to confirm her thoughts once and for all, her father spoke again.

This time she *did* detect a few tears glistening in his eyes.

And she certainly sensed the underlying tremble to his voice.

"Your mother and I always loved you *so* much." He shook his head and then blinked several times. If this was an effort to clear the tears from his eyes then the gesture only succeeded in making his eyes all the more damp; and his tears all the more pronounced. "We made mistakes, we understand that. We put lots of pressure on you. But we only did it from love; because we wanted you to have a good life." He glanced to Lan's mother. "A *good* life like the one your mother and I were able to provide for you."

Lan felt herself trembling all over now.

A single tear streaked free of the corner of her eye.

And a warmth ran through her gut.

She wondered if she might be able to sneak out of the suite—to go off and be with herself for a little while—but she realised that she was too afraid to do that.

She was afraid that if she left her parents alone they would be gone when she returned. And it felt like they had so much more to speak about. So much 'catching up' to do.

When the silence had settled over the room for perhaps ten minutes or longer, Lan finally got hold of herself; told herself that she needed to remain on task.

That she needed to keep things on *point*.

That was perhaps the only way she might be able to get through this meeting.

She turned her gaze across her parents, the tears still causing her vision to blur at the edges. "Why . . . what . . . *how* did you come here? To the *Moon?*"

Her parents exchanged glances, and—much to Lan's surprise —smiled.

The smiles took Lan more off guard than the tears had done.

In her mind, at least, she had always imagined her parents to be a pair of unshakeable, nothing-but-serious service people. To see this recollection—wrongful or not—being shattered before her own eyes unnerved her.

Actually, it more than unnerved her.

It sent skitters through her stomach.

It made her feel uneasy about her memories.

About *all* of her memories.

Could she ever really tell exactly what was real?

Could she *ever* really relay the exact details of what had occurred in her personal past?

Her parents explained to her, in due course, about the kidnapping threat. About how some terrorist group—hostile to the ROCAF; and to China in general—had realised Lan's globe-trotting ways. That their communications had been intercepted, and their intentions discovered, but their location never quite pinned down. Of course, all along, the government had known all about Lan's current location; her current employ being Celestial Stays, based on the Moon.

There had been a series of meetings with Lan's parents in which they had gone through the various threats, and where they had finally decided upon a satisfactory conclusion.

A way to keep both Lan, and the government, free of any potential threat.

They had decided to release the story about Lan being killed en route to the Moon.

Lan studied her parents' tone of voice as they relayed this information.

The way that they explained this whole situation was so calm . . . and her father—apparently noting this for himself—finally remarked on it.

"I know this must all sound so *matter-of-fact*," he said. "This must all sound as if it is just a normal, everyday occurrence." He glanced to Lan's mother, and then back to Lan herself. "But what you must understand is that we believed you were gone—that you were gone for *good*. We saw no reason to contact you. We did not want to ruin the happiness which you had surely found on your travels."

Lan thought about her perceived 'happiness'.

Had she been happy?

Had it made her happier to be far from her parents . . . from her own culture?

Or had she just told herself there was no way back?

Her father continued, "We believed that it was in congruence with everyone's wishes that you should be allowed to *die* . . . at least in the media outlets." He glanced again to Lan's mother, clearly uneasy with this even now; after the decision had been made. "We wanted it so that you could have a fresh start; so that you would not be held back by your past." He paused for a long moment, then added, "By your parents."

Lan felt the tears again beginning to well up in the corners of her eyes.

Again, she pushed them down.

It was tragic, she thought, *tragic* that she had allowed herself to believe that her parents were uncaring for so long . . . only now did she realise that, most likely—buried deep down, and forgotten—it'd been some form of coping mechanism.

A means for her to *lie* herself into believing her parents really had disowned her.

When nothing could've been further from the truth . . .

Lan's mother picked up the slack in the conversation. "We knew that it would not be a permanent solution. We believed that there might well be some *friction* from the Celestial Stays company. That the story would soon not be believed. But it was only supposed to be a temporary solution; to keep you safe." She glanced to Lan's father. "And to give us some peace of mind."

Lan allowed the words to hang in the air a few seconds, then said, "What did you plan on doing when I returned? When it was made obvious that I was not dead?"

Her parents exchanged glances.

Her mother spoke.

"We would have met with you then," she said, her voice crisp and cool. "We would have told you the truth—about what we had to do for your safety and our own."

There was a momentary pause.

"And what then?" Lan asked.

"Well," her mother replied, then trailed off, again exchanging glances with her father. "We believe that we would have reached the same conclusion."

"And what conclusion is that?"

Her mother eyed her closely.

For a second, Lan felt as if they were all back home—back in their apartment in Shanghai; above Huashan Park. She thought of how she would often look through the windows steamed up with condensation; down to those who skittered about the park far below; as busy as ants. And she thought about what her mother and father would often tell her about the importance of being occupied; of being *told* what to do. Otherwise the world would be *chaos*.

"Your father and I," her mother began, "we decided to retire."

For the longest time Lan simply couldn't absorb the impact of what her mother said.

It was like someone had punched her in the chest.

She actually felt a pang of pain through her cracked rib.

"What?"

Her mother looked out the window; across the lunar plains. "That was one of the conditions."

"One of the conditions of *what*?"

"One of the conditions of sending us to the Moon."

Lan frowned, then met her mother's gaze. She saw a Shuttle flying out of the Hangar; soaring across the dust. She knew that it would be Patrick piloting the Shuttle; that ever since Gofreddo had been suspended from duty, he had taken up the slack. It was almost a masochistic move; as if he needed to punish himself for his perceived 'betrayal' of his friend.

Finally, Lan turned back to her mother, realising that she was now eyeing her closely. Lan knew that she had to ask the question.

So she did.

"Why *did* you come to the Moon?" she asked. "Why did the government send you here?"

Her mother's slight smile slipped from her lips. She glanced back to Lan's father, then said, "The government sent us here to bring you home."

Lan felt herself sinking.

Quickly.

Without control.

She almost lost herself to the blackness.

But—*somehow*—held herself back from the brink.

NON-STANDARD PROTOCOL

*P*atrick *had reached* the stage of the trip where the Shuttle had simply become an extension of himself. When his body had melted away and he and the ship had become one.

It had been a standard flight—much like any other—and he was looking forward to getting back to the Hangar; to stripping off his flight suit and ducking his head beneath a hot shower. He supposed that it should blow his mind that it was even possible for him to take a hot shower on the Moon, but there were some days when he took such wonders for granted.

It was strange how quickly he could adapt.

How quickly things became *normal*.

As he inched his fingers across the touchscreen which affected the reverse thrusters, he found himself thinking about Lan; and thinking to himself that he could never imagine an eventuality where *she* became 'normal'. It seemed that every time they came into contact whole new branches of reality—all of them previously unseen; unconsidered—came into being.

Whenever he passed by a mirror, inspected himself in it, he surprised himself to see that he was smiling widely. He would never have believed that he had been missing something. On the surface of things, he had been happy with his life.

With who he was.

But there *had* been something missing.

There had been *someone* missing.

And that person, that someone, was Lan Niu.

Patrick felt the gentle, familiar rumble of the reverse thrusters pumping through his chair. He eyed the opening in the Shuttle Hangar up ahead. He cast a quick glance back over his shoulder, to his passengers. It was a couple from Kazakhstan. And although in the past he would've rolled his eyes at the prospect of having to be a third wheel for some coupley, romantic, lovey-dovey outing, he had found that today he hadn't minded much. He had even smiled on them when he had felt nothing but awkwardness; about being there to cramp their style ... to get in the way of their embraces and their kisses.

Patrick eyed the opening to the Hangar now.

His whole body felt strangely light.

Weird things had come over him ever since he'd met Lan.

Suddenly all those love songs he'd heard throughout life made sense.

More than a few times, he'd woken up in the middle of the night and found that his heart was pounding for no discernible reason.

And then he saw her face in his mind's eye.

And he knew the reason.

He first realised there was something wrong when he caught

the blinking red light out of the corner of his eye. He didn't have time to register just which component it referred to; only to realise that the Shuttle was dropping.

And *fast*.

He jabbed his fingers down on the touchscreen.

An alarm peeped into his inner earpiece.

Over his shoulder, he was dimly aware of his passengers shouting out.

He pulled back on the controls.

Tried to bring the Shuttle nose back up.

To bring the lagging craft into the Hangar.

But it was too late.

Too late.

Because there was nothing else he could do, he continued to yank back on the controls.

To *try* and bring the nose back up.

And he felt the whole craft continue to sink.

To lose its tail.

As he blacked out, he caught sight of the Earth.

Twirling away above.

Its beautiful, greeny-blue glow.

Would he ever see it again?

THE BLUE MOON SUITE

*L*an *was still reeling* from what her parents had told her—
that they had travelled all the way to the Moon so that
they might take her back with them to Earth—when she
observed, through the window of the Blue Moon Suite, the Shuttle
lagging as it floated into the Hangar.

Lan's parents too—the two of them having been aviators from
an early age—had been tracking the sight. It seemed as if all three
of them had noticed the Shuttle had got itself into trouble; that it
wasn't going to be anything like a routine landing. Still, it was
surreal to see the Shuttle sink backward—its nose pointed up into
space; toward the Earth—and for it to drop down, landing on the
lunar plains with a heavy impact. And then the alarms started up.

. . . Or Lan *thought* they were alarms.

She believed the sound came from the Link.

But she soon realised that it was just a ringing in her ears.

That she was in shock.

And yet she acted quickly, without thinking.

She heard her parents calling out after her, demanding that she return. Though how they could possibly believe that—*after all these years*—they would be able to order her around, that she would actually obey what they demanded she do, escaped her.

She made it out into the corridor, and then down in the lift.

She evaded Mackenzie when she appeared between the closing lift doors, apparently arriving on the scene because of her parents' cries.

When she got down to the lobby of the Lunar Grand, she expected Mackenzie to have alerted someone—to have sent someone after her—but there was no one to stop Lan from getting out through the doors of the hotel and leaping into the recently arrived PEAR.

She made it to the Shuttle Hangar in time to see the emergency crews—one of the Infirmary PEARs—taking off. She watched on, powerless, as it tore through the air above her head, directed for the Infirmary.

When Lan turned back, she saw that the PEAR she had arrived to the Shuttle Hangar in had departed; that it had been called away to another landing pad. She wondered what to do for a fraction of a second and then settled for entering the Shuttle Hangar itself.

It was here that she found herself nose to nose with her boss.

With Supervisor Duval.

He blocked her path, dressed in his jet-black Security Division overalls; just as Lan herself was dressed. She eyed the blaster pistol he wore down at his thigh, and how his hand hovered over the grip, ready to draw it out at a moment's notice.

"Where you think you're going, Niu?" he asked, his voice firm, *no-nonsense*.

"Was Patrick . . . was Patrick *Fourie* in that Shuttle?"

Duval pouted, clearly unwilling to give away any information.

Despite everything—despite the fact that the man she *loved* might be in peril—she respected Duval's dedication to his job. He never allowed sentiment to impede his judgement.

Becoming exasperated now, she stared Duval sharply in the eye. "Was anyone injured? Anyone *killed?*"

Duval held himself very still. Then he looked off over her head into the middle distance.

Lan took the opportunity to gaze beyond him, into the Shuttle Hangar.

There she made out a couple, the two of them being attended to by medics.

No sign of Patrick.

Which suggested he—or someone *else*—had been taken away in that PEAR.

Realising that it was the best she had to go on, Lan turned her attention to the departing PEAR.

She needed to go after it . . . to the Infirmary.

There was no other option.

And she had to move quickly.

There was no way she was going to allow her parents to steal her away from here without her finding out what'd happened to Patrick; the only man she had ever loved.

And perhaps the only man she *would* ever love.

Another PEAR arrived to the landing pad.

She leaped inside.

Headed to the Infirmary.

––––––––––

There was more Security at the Infirmary.

Lan managed to meander her way through the crowds.

Everything seemed to be in a state of panic.

This wasn't supposed to happen beneath the Celestial Stays Dome.

Problems—*accidents*—were not allowed.

That was one of the most famous loglines.

The well-known phrases used to sell the lunar experience:

Safer than intercontinental air travel.

As Lan pressed herself up against the wall, feeling her ribs aching from where she'd cracked one of them, she found all kinds of strange thoughts flashing into her mind.

Who had come up with that particular tagline?

Who had thought that rich people—the sort who could afford the trip to the Celestial Stays Dome—would wish for assurances that it was safer than intercontinental air travel?

. . . But someone *had* thought of it.

Lan finally reached a dead-end on one of the upper floors.

She found herself facing off with a member of the Security Division.

A balding head of red hair.

Freckles covering both cheeks.

And rancid, stinking breath of fish guts.

Of course she knew the person.

Beneath his flag—*the United Kingdom*—she read off his nametag: D. Teeson

It was a guy called David Teeson . . . but he went by 'Dave' to all his friends.

Lan had had several run-ins with David Teeson.

Mostly it was down to his attempts at humour. He was one of those overgrown children who'd never quite realised that the idea of putting strange and unexpected items in personal lockers wasn't funny. And one day, Lan had snapped.

She recalled 'Dave' and his cronies standing off to one side in the locker rooms as she'd opened up her locker, only to have several dozens of eggs roll out and splatter at her feet. Perhaps Lan might've been able to see the funny side—*perhaps*—if none of the egg had got onto her uniform, but, as it was, one of the largest of the eggs undid itself all over her nametag.

She had spun around so fast that she could still recall—to this very day—the beleaguered expression on Dave's face. She had rushed up to him, grabbing him by the throat, lifting him clean up and off his feet, before pinning him to a locker on the opposite side of the room.

At any moment, Lan had expected to feel the steady grasp of one of his cronies; ready to come to Dave's aid to save him from this crazy woman.

But not one of them stepped in.

And as Lan had tightened her grip on his throat, she had stared into his eyes. She was certain that she'd *seen* his eyes bulge from their sockets. She believed she'd heard him croak out a plea to her through his sealed throat . . . *praying* for his life.

Looking back, that was—*perhaps*—the only reason she'd allowed him to drop.

The only reason why she hadn't followed through.

Because, and there was no doubt about it, she had been prepared to kill him right there and then. In that moment—in that moment of white, hot rage.

And now, as the two of them eyeballed one another, as Dave blocked her path, she wondered if she shouldn't have done just that.

At least then she never would've met Patrick.

And they never would've met *right now*.

Patrick smeared on a smirk. "Just got word," he said, reaching for the blaster stuck into his thigh holster. "There's a warrant out for one Lan Niu." He flipped a glance at her name, sewn on at her breast pocket, as if he didn't already know it. "Guess that must be you, huh?"

Lan glanced back over her shoulder.

No one.

He seemed to be alone.

She turned back, looked Dave over.

He didn't seem to be too perplexed by the task facing him . . . but, then again, he was armed; and she was a *woman*. She supposed that these two facts changed everything about the past positions they'd held; what with her pinning him up against a locker, strangling the life out of him with her bare hands. Well, one thing was for certain, he was in for a shock.

When he reached for the blaster, Lan was quick.

She grabbed his wrist, yanked it wide, and *slammed* it against the wall.

He let out a *yowl*.

The blaster dropped at their feet with a clatter.

He swore under his breath, grabbing his injured wrist.

He doubled over himself.

Stared up at her with a scowl fixed on his face.

"You *bitch!*" he roared.

The volume of his voice took Lan back for a second.

She had to remind herself of what'd transpired before.

How she had fought him *off* before.

And she would do so again.

Her future with Patrick depended on it—it depended on *her*.

Dave took several lungfuls of air, apparently pumping himself up, then he flew at her.

Acting quickly, Lan sidestepped, and then—with no technique;

only the pure force which many weights sessions could achieve—she brought her fists down upon his back.

He lost his balance.

Dropped to the floor with a cry.

She stood and stared down at him for several moments, wondering just at what she had done, and what consequences it would surely have.

Just as Dave began to stir from where he lay, Lan rushed off along the corridor.

As Lan bolted along the corridor, her mind fizzing with mad thoughts as she attempted to get her brain around what had just happened—that Patrick might be in mortal peril—she noted a series of white lab coats, all of them hanging off pegs in an alcove.

She glanced about her, and noticing that she was alone, she dashed into the alcove; hooked one of the coats off its peg and shrugged it on over her shoulders.

Feeling that she at least had the semblance of a disguise now, she headed back out into the corridor. She ventured onward.

She finally centred upon a group of obviously busy medics.

In a hurried voice which came as a natural extension of her disguise, she asked them what'd become of the patient . . . where he was.

She was half stunned when they told her exactly where he was.

When they pointed her off along the corridor.

Another few doors away.

Lan hurried her way onward.

Determined now.

Unstoppable now.

She kept on her way . . . feeling each step drawing her closer . . . her ribs tingled with pain . . . a searing heat ran through her blood . . . her thoughts came to her in dribs and drabs.

She paced onward, past the seemingly endless doors, until she reached the one which the medics had indicated was where the patient was being cared for. Where *Patrick* was being cared for.

Lan stood before the door for a the longest moment. She tried to compose herself. To get her breathing back under control. Then she jabbed the button beside the door.

And it slid back into the wall.

Before her stood Alicia and Louise.

The two of them staring her down.

Blocking her path.

As the two of them grabbed hold of her arms, she struggled. She nearly threw them off completely. She nearly managed to put her strength to work; to toss the two of them aside. But her ribs throbbed, and her mind felt ragged and torn.

While Alicia and Louise wrestled her to the ground, she heard familiar snatches of shouting voices. The Security Division. They were here. The ones that Dave had called.

Even though Lan felt the pain wracking her entire body now, she managed to thrust herself upward for one final time. To make one last effort.

As the stomping boots filled her hearing, she managed to force herself onto one knee, and to see through the door ahead of her. There was a curtain. It was drawn.

The royal blue of Celestial Stays.

Right as Alicia and Louise bore down on her, threatening to snuff out any hope she had at peripheral vision, the curtain swished back . . . a medic coming through.

And she managed to catch a snatch of the sight within.

She saw Patrick's face.

His whole body.

Tucked up in the hospital bed.

Wires . . . tubes . . . *humming* . . .

And she heard his voice . . . her supervisor . . . *Duval's* voice.

"Take her away!"

34

WAIT PERIOD

*an was taken to Security HQ—to one of the lockups there.
To be honest, she didn't have all that much reason to
complain. When she compared the lockup to all the
lockups she'd been familiar with back on Earth—in the other security jobs she'd worked—it was like a five-star hotel suite . . . not
quite the Blue Moon Suite, but *still* . . .

There was a bed, complete with linen; and there was a small,
circular table and a pair of chairs.

All this furniture was basic, of course. This wasn't meant to be
a special place but it was supposed to meet a certain minimum
level of comfort to which the Celestial Stays Clientele were accustomed. Lan supposed it met with wealthy people's concept of what
jail was.

Her whole body ached.

Although the members of the Security team who'd escorted her
out of the Infirmary had taken pains to be gentle with her, they
had been forced to use their strength when Lan had fought back

against them. She recalled how she had counted out twenty steps from the room in which they kept Patrick until something inside her had snapped. And she had attempted to break free of her captors.

It was then that they'd had to use more force.

When they'd had to yank her off her feet and carry her between them in a tight, unmovable embrace.

She was sitting on the bed now, with her knees tucked up into her chest. She felt the unpleasant throb passing through her ribs and she wondered if the manner in which she'd left the Infirmary had worsened her injuries. Of course, Duval had known about the extent of her injuries; the medic who had demanded that Lan be restricted to light duties would've filed a full status report as a matter of protocol. Duval needed to know how far he could rely upon his inferiors.

And—*apparently*—it served only as bonus information for when said inferiors became hostiles. Just as Lan had done.

The lights in the lockup were bright, and Lan half shut her eyelids to keep herself from becoming blinded. She had no real concept of how long she'd been in the lockup; only that when she had arrived here—when she had been *dragged* in here—she had soon collapsed onto the bed; fallen into something like sleep. She had no recollection of anything but blackness.

Outside, she was aware of footsteps.

A gentle tread.

It was almost like she could never switch off the part of her brain which was constantly tuned into her surroundings —*constantly* taking note of what was going on around her.

Judging it for its level of threat.

There was a *beep* of approval from somewhere, and the door to the lockup swept back into the wall. She took in the group of figures standing in the doorway. However bright the light in the lockup itself happened to be, it seemed as if the light out in the corridor was only brighter still.

She had trouble even *counting* the figures standing in the doorway.

The figures looking in on her.

Soon, though, their faces came clear.

She made out her parents: her mother and father.

And then, at their heels, Mackenzie Angliss.

Further back—*standing behind them all*—was Duval.

Her boss . . .

As she cast her mind back, she had a recollection of snatching for his throat while she had been lugged away from Patrick's hospital room. She hadn't been able to take hold of him, but she felt as if the surprised—*disgusted*—expression on his face had become scarred upon her mind's eye.

Slowly, her parents' voices . . . her *mother's* voice . . . came to her hearing.

"Lan," she said, "we wanted this to be peaceful . . . we wanted you to come quietly. We did not wish to cause a fuss."

Lan felt her whole body go rigid. She didn't understand . . . she didn't understand *anything*.

Then her mind skimmed back; back to the conversation she had shared with her parents in the Blue Moon Suite. She recalled that they had travelled up to the Moon; that they had come to *see her* . . . but why . . . *why* had it been? The answer to that question soon hit her.

That her parents had told her she was to go home with them.

That she was to go 'home' with them . . .

After fifteen years of constant globe-trotting, could she honestly say she even had a home anymore? She had travelled from job to job; the greatest strength on her CV always being her ability to take only what she needed and to leave behind nothing but glowing references for the professional work she had done.

She thought back to the Shuttle crash; the one which she had witnessed up in the Blue Moon Suite. How it had all happened in slow motion before her very eyes. And how she had realised—even while she was watching—that it was Patrick who was implicated.

She switched her attention back to the present moment.

When she spoke, her voice felt floaty—somehow as if it was emerging from her mouth via some ether; through some other consciousness. Some other reality.

"You came up here—to the *Moon*—because the government want me back on Earth . . . is that correct?"

Her mother remained very still.

Lan wondered if she was going to deny this.

She shifted her attention onto her father, then onto Mackenzie Angliss, and to Duval, the two of them standing in the background; almost ashamed to be present.

But Lan supposed that protocol demanded they *were* present.

So that Lan might not kill her own parents with her bare hands.

Finally, her mother nodded by way of reply.

Lan turned her attention onto Duval, and onto Mackenzie. "And you two are here to ensure that I go with them? That I get on the next Shuttle back to Earth?"

Neither of them said anything or reacted in any way.

But it didn't matter, their silence spoke volumes.

Feeling her thoughts once again becoming settled—her brain finally slowing itself down so that she could hear its constant imaginings—Lan focussed back onto her mother.

"When do you plan on taking me?" she asked. "When do I have to go?"

Her mother remained silent for the longest time, and Lan convinced herself that she was going to say nothing; that she was —in some way—going to *pull rank* . . . as Lan had so often seen it when she'd been a child. Her parents were correct because they were her *parents*.

Her mother did speak up at last, however.

"The Shuttle leaves later today," she said. "And we shall *all* be on it."

Lan felt as if the world was slipping away from her once again.

But the harsh, stabbing pain in her ribs brought her back to the present.

The pain *pinned* her to reality.

However much she would've liked to escape to fantasy.

35

RECUPERATION

*P*atrick *was aware* of various bots and droids whirring around him.

It was strange.

To begin with, he only saw them in his mind.

Blurred, childlike images of their machine components; their glistening bodywork; the rubber hoses jutting out from here, plugging into that spot *there* . . .

It seemed to take a monumental force for him to so much as crack open a single eyelid.

And, when he did, the world continued to be blurred before him.

He eyed the bots and droids; took in their bright, blinking lights. And he noted the forms off to the outer edges of the room. He recognised who they were by their lab coats . . . by the long white coats they wore. And then there was another pair of figures.

Standing in the doorway.

Blocking the light from the corridor.

He blinked once.

Twice.

And his brain became clearer.

He turned his thoughts back to the crash . . . to how he had been closing in on the Shuttle Hangar . . . and how he'd been bringing her in so slowly—so gently . . . all of those practised motions which he had perfected over time. The movements which'd become second nature to him as a Shuttle pilot. And then . . . and then . . . it'd all . . . *gone away.*

The last thing he recalled was the Shuttle sinking backward, and the sound of the failing thrusters, and the blazing sun in the sky beating down upon him.

It had sent him back to a time in his childhood; a time when he'd visited the beach . . . and those lapping waves . . . those *screeching* gulls . . . the sounds of laughter and animated conversation all around . . . and then . . . and then . . .

It'd all been replaced by bleeping.

The *bleeping* he heard right now.

All around.

When Patrick attempted to lift himself up in bed, he felt a severe pain dance down his spine. His stomach crunched in on itself. And his skull squeezed his brain.

He gave up the effort, feeling himself winded from such a simple attempted action.

All his nerves seemed to be tingling.

He felt tense and relaxed—all at the same time.

Where was he . . . where *was* he?

And then the voices came.

"Pat? . . . Pat?"

It took a moment for Patrick to fully recognise the voice.

And he heard the familiar smile there.

"*¿Qué haces?*"

Patrick felt a smile sneak onto his lips before he really knew why.

Before he *really* was able to consciously realise the voice was Gofreddo's.

That Gofreddo was with him.

Where he was with him, Patrick couldn't say for certain.

It was then that he felt a steady touch on his shoulder.

"Oh, Patrick."

That steady, no-nonsense, Midwestern accent.

Alicia.

Alicia Brennan.

Patrick searched his mind, trying to recover his bearings; to work out just what was going on here . . . and what role he played in proceedings.

He felt as if something was wrong.

As if *he* had done something *wrong.*

He thought back to the crash . . . because that was what it had been, hadn't it?

. . . Why else was he here?

But, no, there was something else, too.

Something *else.*

Then, all at once, he recalled.

How he had gone to Mackenzie Angliss.

Informed her of Gofreddo's negligence.

How he had been making simple mistakes.

Simple but *costly* mistakes.

When Patrick first managed to form words, though, he stuck to the more recent past. "The passengers," he said, his voice inexplicably gruff . . . *dry.* "Are they . . ."

He felt Alicia grip his shoulder; give it a squeeze.

"They're fine," she said. "You have nothing to worry about."

A tension which'd existed at the back of Patrick's mind all of a sudden eased. He realised that his passengers' wellbeing had been foremost in his thoughts. He wondered what he might've done to himself if he'd heard that something had befallen them; that they had come to some harm because of a lack of his skill. Because of an error of *his* judgement.

That weight off his mind for the time being, he turned his attention onto Gofreddo.

This was the first time they had spoken since Patrick had gone to Mackenzie; since he had told her of his fears. It was somewhat surreal to see Gofreddo smiling back at him.

Beaming, really . . . from ear to ear.

"I . . . I'm *sorry*," Patrick just about got out, fumbling his words; the weakness which currently wracked his body coming to the fore.

"Do not worry," Gofreddo replied, that same smile in his voice. "You did what you needed to do." He held up his hands, as if in surrender somehow. "In fact, some might say you are a hero."

Patrick held himself still. He took pains to breathe in deeply, to try and bring his mind back to the sharpness it had possessed before the crash. "What . . . what was the reason? . . . What was the *fault?*"

Here Patrick felt a tension enter the atmosphere.

He realised that—had these been other circumstances; had he been anywhere else other than a hospital bed after having made a miraculous recovery—he would never have brought the matter up. Not so soon after the crash, in any case. He supposed that his sense of politeness—his lightness of foot when it came to considering the feelings of others—had been thrown out of whack by the crash, and whatever sedatives the medics had been dripping into his body.

But Gofreddo answered all the same. "It is early still," Gofreddo said, "but it is believed to be a failure in the Shuttle's systems; in some of the *code* . . ."

Patrick felt the words linger in the air.

The *uncertainty.*

Could Patrick ever be sure that the Celestial Stays administration would tell the truth where Gofreddo Zito was concerned?

All the same, Patrick felt glad to have his best friend back.

And to be able to speak with him freely seemed almost like an undeserved bonus.

"Well," Alicia said, "I guess I'll leave you two alone to get all caught up, all righty?"

Although she phrased this as a question, she was making for the door before Patrick or Gofreddo had the chance to reply.

The room coming clear now—and Patrick's actual surroundings; complete with the various droids, bots and medics hovering about his bedside—he shifted his attention onto Gofreddo himself. As he had appeared to Patrick throughout the past few weeks, Gofreddo looked ragged, overworked as if he had something on his mind.

Patrick was on the cusp of asking just what it was when he recalled the conversation they had had what seemed *weeks* ago . . . now that he thought of it, he wasn't entirely sure whether or not it'd just been a dream. And maybe it was for this reason that Patrick found himself striking a light-hearted tone when he addressed the point. "I guess this disqualifies me from the mission."

Gofreddo's smile faltered for a moment; a slight reaction which told Patrick—*unambiguously*—that he was treading on thin ice . . .

that he was taking liberties with his friend's feelings . . . threatening to stomp on his innermost dreams.

Finally, though, when Patrick was surest that Gofreddo would simply turn on his heel and storm from the room, he broke out his familiar smile. "Far from it," he said. "In fact, I would say that it does nothing but *confirm* your suitability for the mission . . . what with your handling of that crash; why *wouldn't* I wish for a pilot of your ability?" Here he broke off his gaze with Patrick, his eyes sinking in their sockets so that his focus turned to the toes of his boots. "I suppose the *real* question should be whether or not you trust me."

All of a sudden, Patrick felt as if the room was spinning.

His heart beat against his ribs.

And he felt a sucking, nauseous feeling enter his blood.

"I . . . of course . . . I *trust* you," Patrick managed to get out. And then, feeling a ticklish sensation in the pit of his gut, he added, "As long as you leave the mechanical work to me."

Gofreddo let out a booming laugh.

One of those infectious, impossible-to-ignore bouts of laughter which Patrick had come to recognise as one of Gofreddo Zito's trademarks. When he got himself back under control, he bowed his head, still smiling, then said, "I believe my time is up . . . if I do not obey the rules I'm sure that they"—he jerked his thumb over his shoulder to indicate the medics, bots and droids—"will throw me out." Without another word, Gofreddo began to head for the door.

Patrick spoke out, stopping him in his tracks.

"Lan?" he said, and then, realising that he'd only spoken her name—that he had failed to elaborate—he wondered if he should do so.

But it seemed Gofreddo caught what he'd implied.

Turning back to him, a slight wince now scarring his lips, Gofreddo said, "I . . . I think you had better speak with *Mackenzie* about that . . ." And then, with a vague smile, he vanished off through the doorway. Padding along the corridor.

Patrick felt a throb in the pit of his stomach.

And—soon enough—it became an almost unshiftable *hum*.

Like electricity.

As if a ball of lightning had spontaneously come into being within him.

It was with this energy coursing through his veins that he propped himself up in bed.

One of the droids trudged over to him; recommended that he lie himself back down.

But Patrick ignored the request.

Soon enough, the medics, too, had turned their attention onto him.

Patrick was already sat on the edge of the hospital bed now, though.

And he had unhooked himself from the machines around him.

With a single glance, he eyed the doorway—the light flooding in from outside; from the Celestial Stays Dome—and he broke into a run.

As he sprinted down the corridors, he seemed to find fresh energy—*fresh vigour*—from somewhere. He felt the draught blowing up his backless hospital gown.

But he didn't care.

He was going to find her.

Even if it *killed* him to do so.

36

EXIT PROCEDURES

*L*an *was deeply aware* of the pair of security guards flanking her.

Both of them had their blasters drawn.

One of them was Dave, the guard she had flattened back at the Infirmary.

The other was Duval.

Her boss . . . or should that be *ex*-boss?

Her parents trudged before her, the two of them—like herself—wearing the grey-white flight overalls assigned to those on the outside of the Dome; those who were either arriving, or leaving, or—like Patrick—caught somewhere between.

Throughout this whole experience, Lan had cottoned onto the idea that there were forces more sizeable—more *considerable*—than Celestial Stays at work here.

It seemed as if the world had turned against her.

As if the world had turned against her *and* Patrick.

It was so cruel that they had found one another, only to be torn apart at the first opportunity.

Lan hadn't even been permitted to visit his hospital room; to bid him goodbye.

She had merely been frogmarched by Dave and Duval, her parents neatly striding before her, toward the Rover Pool; where they would take a Rover out to the Launch Site.

The place where Lan was destined to make her farewell to the lunar surface.

It was such an anti-climax.

It felt as if there was still so much left undone.

Lan *still* had had so much to give to Celestial Stays.

. . . So much to give to Patrick.

And she couldn't even say goodbye.

Couldn't *even* say goodbye.

She glanced back over her shoulder, as if she had somehow managed to convince herself that the Security standing on her heels would've disappeared.

On the way here—in the PEAR—her mother had hurriedly explained how the government would be waiting for them when they landed back on Earth. And that Lan was to cooperate.

They wanted to know everything about her.

About what she'd been doing these past years.

And then, as Lan had been told, she was to be turned over to their 'protection'.

Lan had no pretences surrounding the government's true intent. She knew that, if she got on that Shuttle with her parents, if she was turned over into the 'care' of the government officials waiting for her, that she would become a life-long prisoner. Oh, she might be permitted to even live at home. But she would—*never again*—be permitted to leave her city.

The very thought of being trapped in the same space as her parents—the very ones who had betrayed her—tasted bitter in her throat. And yet, what was she supposed to do?

"Keep moving," Duval said, uttering the order beneath his breath. "We're almost there."

Lan tested his patience a second or so more, but dared not to press him any further. She knew enough about her boss that she didn't doubt his capabilities to act when he really had to . . . to take the action which *needed* to be taken.

As she continued on her way, she was surprised to find her mother falling back from her father, and beginning to pace alongside her. Lan didn't turn to look when her mother began to speak.

If she could help it, she would never look at her mother again.

"You must appreciate the seriousness of the situation, Lan. There is no pathway for you—no way for you to steer clear of the government while on Earth . . . as you know, there are representatives all over the globe." She paused for a long moment, and Lan hoped that she would just shut up completely. But she kept going. "You must understand that the situation is hopeless; that your best option is to cooperate . . . to do *just* as they say."

Lan had the urge to scream out; to tell her to *shut up*!

But she just couldn't find the strength.

Somewhere—*somehow*—a voice within her told her that she needed to bide her time.

That she needed to conserve her energy.

If she got one final chance then she needed to be ready.

Although, on the face of the situation—from the fact that she was being held under close observation by Duval—she knew that it would be extremely unlikely she *would* get a chance; any chance at all.

As they continued on their way, the Rovers all coming into

view now, her mother continued to speak. "Of course, the only place where you could remain without their capture . . . without their agents easily being able to get hold of you would be here." Again, she paused. "The *Moon*."

Lan's eyeballs nearly rolled cleaned out of their sockets.

She stared long and hard at her mother.

Her concentration was only broken by Duval's stern reprimand.

For her to, *Get a move on!*

After she'd taken a second to fully absorb her mother's meaning, she did as Duval said.

Her thoughts came quickly. It reminded her of a time when she had served as security for an oil refinery based up in Alaska. She recalled how she had looked out of the window one day and seen a blizzard flurrying past; rapidly collecting into snowdrifts.

It'd been chaos.

Impossible to separate one snowflake from the next.

And that was just how her thoughts felt now.

She saw the Rovers, and she felt Duval and Dave on her heels.

If she was going to do something then . . . it *had* to be now.

Duval was the one who seemed to read her mind.

Dave, though, was his usual, slow, dim-witted self.

Later, Lan speculated as to whether Duval's prime mistake had been to select a member of the Security Division who was obviously so *oblivious*.

Her movement was near instantaneous.

She brought her arm down *hard* on Dave's wrist.

Heard a stomach-wrenching *crunch*.

His blaster tumbled free of his grip.

Lan caught it before it hit the floor.

Then—*acting on instinct*—she dived to one side.

An impossibly warm heat seared her cheek.

She smelled burned hair.

But she forced herself back up.

Back onto her feet.

She hurtled herself behind a nearby pillar.

Allowed herself a second or two so that she might regain her breath.

Then, catching Duval in her sights, she let loose a flurry of fire from the blaster.

She saw him drop to the floor.

But she didn't quite believe it.

Dave—she saw—was holding his hands up . . . his palms facing her.

Surrendering.

She switched her attention back onto Duval—still on the ground, and now clutching his left leg, teeth gritted, writhing in apparent agony. "You *bitch*!" he called out. "You little *bitch*!"

Lan paid him no mind.

She was well used to such remarks when she bested men.

She had become so used to beating them at their own games— at brute strength; at shows of extreme violence—that the wrath she incurred seemed only part and parcel.

She burst out of cover, quickly trotting up to Duval, kicking the blaster far from where it'd fallen onto the ground. Then she instructed Dave to sit beside Duval.

Next, she turned to her parents. "Go!" she said, her voice wavering now; for the first time, the fatigue which'd wracked her body becoming obvious in her voice.

Neither of her parents moved.

They both seemed . . . *stunned.*

Their mouths formed 'oh' shapes.

Lan felt a tear run down her cheek.

With her free hand—the hand which didn't hold the blaster—she wiped it clean.

"*Go!*" she repeated, this time with her voice cracking completely.

Again, neither of her parents moved.

They seemed rooted to the spot.

"You're leaving me behind!" Lan shouted at them, as if they hadn't heard a word she'd said.

Her mother remained still, then Lan noticed the tears coming to her eyes.

They trickled down her cheeks.

"We love you, Lan," she said. "You must know that."

Lan felt something tremble within her.

She wasn't sure what it was . . . or if she could control it.

So she was forced to turn her mind back to the matter at hand.

The *blaster* she held down at her side.

"Please," Lan said; this time with a weak voice. "Go, now."

She felt her mother take hold of her free hand.

She interlocked her fingers with Lan's.

Gave her hand a squeeze.

Then she reached around Lan, and hugged her to her chest.

When she drew Lan close enough to whisper in her ear, she said, "Take care, my darling—we shall be there for you always."

It felt like the last time she would ever see her mother when she released her from her grip. And then, when she turned her attention onto her father, and he did the same—embracing her as her mother had embraced her—she knew it was the last time she would ever see her father too . . .

She watched them go—watched them *follow* her orders.

And she wondered what would become of them.

Had they sacrificed themselves for her?

... Or was it that they had already *been* sacrificed?

Had they been strong-armed into taking retirement, and kept on—allowed a degree of freedom—only so that they might bring their daughter back with them?

Lan supposed that she would never truly know.

As her parents clambered into the Rover, she met their eyes, and she could see them both openly crying. The Rover was driven by a bot, and once its pair of passengers was in place, its visor wound down and it took off—out through the airlock, and across the lunar plains.

To the Launch Site.

Despite everything—despite knowing she needed to *run*—Lan stood where she was, unable to find the will to keep on going; to keep on *escaping*.

Because what possible place could she escape *to*?

What her mother had told her was the truth; the government had the entire Earth in its firm grasp. There was nowhere on its green-and-blue surface where Lan could run and be safe from their agents ... from their *influence*.

No, the only place where she could be safe now was the Moon.

Beneath the Celestial Stays Dome.

———

When Lan turned her attention back to the present—to Duval lying on the floor, groaning away, and to Dave who was slouched beside him, staring off into mid-air, as if he had received a blow to the head—her thoughts became sharper.

More pronounced.

This was it ... *this* was what she had to do.

She strolled past the injured Duval and the dazed Dave, and back out into what made up the larger area of Entry Clearance. It was here that the monumental size of her task struck her.

The whole of the Celestial Stays Dome opened out ahead.

She took in the skyline: the Lunar Grand dominating everything; the Crescent Gardens spiralling through all—a much needed patch of green; and then there was the Basements, the place which, for want of a better word, was probably the only 'home' she had truly had in the past few years.

Her heart beat sombrely—percussively—as she absorbed what she needed to do next.

She had to hide . . . she had to find *somewhere* to hide.

And it couldn't be beneath the floorboards of the Orbital Café, although, granted, she did now have some *extremely pleasant* memories associated with that particular place.

Again, her mind spun out of her grasp, her thoughts spiralling from her control.

She stuck to the steps she needed to take.

The steps which were laid out right before her.

And she felt her whole body go *rigid* at the prospect.

It was then that she saw him.

Peering through the glass from outside; into Entry Clearance.

He was dressed in a hospital gown.

And yet—*somehow*—he still looked ravishing.

Patrick.

RE-ENTRY

*L*an felt herself shaking all over.

She could barely think to place one foot in front of the other.

When she turned, though, when she looked sidelong and met his eye, she saw that Patrick was smiling back at her. And that sent a warmth through her.

A *much-needed* warmth.

On her way here, to meet with Frau Köhler, Lan had got halfway to convincing herself that her body was something like a block of ice; both because of the temperature, and because of its rigid, ungiving texture. She thought that it would take only the slightest of touches to smash her entire *being* into thousands of insignificant fragments.

Mackenzie Angliss had lent Frau Köhler her office for the duration of the scheduled meeting—although 'lent', Lan supposed, was a relative term given that Frau Köhler was the owner of the entirety of Celestial Stays.

Things had happened quickly over the past week—a week since Lan's parents had departed the Moon . . . a week which Lan had expected to spend in hiding.

But it hadn't turned out that way.

Soon after she had left her parents behind—so that they might take the Rover which'd lead them off to the Launch Site—she had run into Patrick just outside the Entry Clearance building. He had come straight from the Infirmary; somehow divining that this was where Lan was located.

That Lan was to be shipped off the face of the Moon.

And sent into the clutches of the waiting governmental forces on the Earth below.

She had told him what she had done . . . how she had disarmed Dave—for the second time that day, no less—and how she had *shot* Duval . . .

And how Lan had done it because of the circumstances.

Because of what awaited her on Earth's surface.

Patrick had surprised her with his air of calm.

How he had been seemingly unflapped by the whole episode.

He had told her that they needed to get in touch with Mackenzie.

That they needed to 'talk things out'—try to *reason* with the Celestial Stays administration. Because, if they didn't do so right away, then they would only bury themselves in deeper trouble.

It had gone against every one of Lan's survival instincts to turn herself in, but she somehow allowed Patrick to convince her. When she thought on it later, she decided that Patrick was likely the only human being alive who would've been *capable* of convincing her.

Lan had expected herself to be taken to another lockup, and, indeed, she had been.

What did she think would happen if she shot the Supervisor of Security?

It was her greatest fear at that point that they would separate her from Patrick.

That they would delay the launch.

That they would *make sure* Lan was on the Shuttle headed back to Earth.

But, as it turned out, they allowed Patrick to stay with her in the lockup . . . and they assured her, after Lan had explained fully to Mackenzie her situation—and after Mackenzie had contacted Frau Köhler; back on Earth—that she wouldn't be subjected to the launch.

It was with great relief that a member of Security showed up later in the evening of Lan's arrest to inform her that the Shuttle had finally left the Moon.

The relief had been fleeting, however.

It had soon been replaced with a sense of loss.

And were there many greater senses of loss than losing a parent —let alone both?

Lan certainly lost herself to grief that night . . .

When she had woken the next morning—gladly lying beside Patrick; and very much *still* on the Moon—she had been informed that Frau Köhler was currently considering her case; and that, in the meantime, Lan would be granted indefinite leave to remain on the Moon.

Beneath the Celestial Stays Dome.

It was probably the one place in the whole of human existence where the government couldn't touch her . . . and, Lan was certain, Frau Köhler understood that better than most.

Lan snapped back to the present.

She looked ahead, to Mackenzie Angliss's office.

The glass walls afforded a view of the occupant at the desk; just as it had the day when Lan had been escorted here by Alicia and Louise. Today, though, it was Frau Köhler.

Lan glanced to Patrick, who looked back at her, giving her a slight nod of encouragement. There could be no turning back now . . . this was the road which Lan had begun upon from the moment she had resisted her parents all those years ago; when she had decided, once and for all, to leave her home behind.

With a deep breath inward, Lan trod through the office doorway.

Lan had once before seen Frau Köhler—*Karolin Köhler*—in the flesh.

And, when she'd done so, it had been at Louise Williams's ceremony; when she had been granted a special award for the bravery she'd shown in seeing off that maniacal ex-boyfriend of hers; Alex Barn.

When Lan had seen her before, Frau Köhler had had her hair clippered short. What little hair that'd remained had been a wheat colour. Now, though, her hair was shoulder-length, and a quite shocking, shimmering silver.

Lan would've thought it a wig, if she hadn't seen work of that quality before . . . if she hadn't seen the sort of marvels with which 'aesthetic' surgery could treat the rich.

Frau Köhler had on a strapless, royal-blue dress which complemented and *accentuated* her sleek, elegant figure. Lan truly believed that she could've been anywhere between thirty and fifty years old; she had the unmistakable—and yet unplaceable—appearance which made her somehow ageless. Lan might not have been too surprised to discover that she had been around for centuries . . . perhaps that was the secret of her raging success in business.

When Frau Köhler spoke, she was surprised that she addressed her not in English—or even *Mandarin*—but in Lan's native Shanghainese.

"It is a pleasure to meet you, Miss Niu."

Although Lan was certain that Frau Köhler's intention in addressing her in her native language was to make her feel at ease, it had almost precisely the opposite effect. Lan was so used to conversing in English—and to only ever speaking with her *parents* in Shanghainese—that she felt close to tears all of a sudden. But she forced the tears away.

She swallowed hard.

And met Frau Köhler's penetrating stare.

Lan couldn't help wondering how many business people—*how many governmental leaders*—Frau Köhler had used that same stare on . . . there had to be *countless* numbers if Frau Köhler's profits for Celestial Stays were anything to go by . . . if the very *feat* of managing to establish a profit-generating enterprise on the Moon had been accomplished.

Lan gently inclined her head. "It is a pleasure to meet you, too, Frau Köhler."

Frau Köhler gave a slight smile at Lan's reply, and then shifted her attention onto Patrick. She spoke to him in a language which Lan didn't recognise at all; but which she supposed to be Patrick's native Afrikaans. She watched on as a similar expression of surprise passed over Patrick's face. In a way it reassured Lan to know that she wasn't the only one in the office who was feeling well out of their comfort zone. Lan glanced back to Frau Köhler.

When Frau Köhler spoke again, it was in English.

Lan supposed this was more of a practical matter than anything else; so that they would have a common language to converse in.

"Now," Frau Köhler said, as if she was seguing effortlessly onto another matter of business, "I'm sure you're well aware of the reason for this meeting." She gave a sly smile. "Having said that, I suppose that I should clarify." She paused a moment, glanced out the window, across the lunar plains, apparently not quite fully over her accomplishments herself; all that she had managed to build here . . . on the *Moon*. "I have been filled in on the details of your, ah . . ." her words trailed off—not because she was searching for the word in English, but because she was working out what would be the best way to phrase it ". . . *condition*."

Here Lan couldn't help but feel a shiver pass around her collar. It was a wonder just how Mackenzie might've communicated her 'condition' to Frau Köhler.

Frau Köhler swallowed; her throat muscles constricting and relaxing. Then she continued, "I know all about the *situation*; the one which brought your parents to the Celestial Stays Dome . . . it *was* the Chinese government, after all, who funded the venture." She drew breath. "It was with a heavy heart that I even accepted the proposal in the first place. I have never been a fan of performing governmental favours whenever it can be avoided. It is far too . . ." again she searched for the word, clearly wanting to put it just right ". . . *complicated* . . . I mean, when it comes to business. It creates too many potential conflicts." She tilted her head to one side; closed one eye as if judging Lan closely. "People get awfully touchy whenever things get *political*—whenever things get *religious* —don't you think?"

Not really knowing how to respond, Lan nodded by way of reply.

When Frau Köhler began to shake her head, Lan wondered if she hadn't been too hasty in nodding. "Bad for business."

Lan felt her chest tighten.

A slight shudder passed through her ribs.

She wondered what was going to happen.

If she was going to be turfed out of the Celestial Stays Dome so simply.

Was Lan 'bad for business'?

As if to assuage Lan's concerns—as if she was capable of reading her mind—Frau Köhler gave a reassuring smile. "Miss Niu," she said, "whatever happens, you must know that I value my employees—and the *welfare* of my employees above all else." She drew breath, her shoulders arching back gracefully as she did so. When she spoke again, her voice had a lighter quality; as if her voice itself was in danger of simply *floating away*. "I've always believed there's something which draws people here; something which *drives* people to take the drastic action of giving up their life on Earth so that they might travel to the Moon. Come to *work* on the Moon." She narrowed her eyes. "Almost something *magnetic*, don't you think?"

Not really knowing *what* to think, Lan met Frau Köhler's stare.

Then, again, nodded back.

"Hmm," Frau Köhler said, folding her hands on top of the desk . . . on top of *Mackenzie Angliss's* desk, "I wonder . . ." Here she glanced to Patrick, then gave him a simple nod.

It seemed that they had already agreed this as some sort of signal that the meeting would be over.

In any case, the gesture was sufficient so that Patrick trudged from the office without another word. Frau Köhler turned her full attention onto Lan. "Now," she said, this time in Shanghainese, "this is how it's going to work—you tell me what you think, all right?"

Lan finally found her voice. "Okay," she said.

A slight smile crawled up one side of Frau Köhler's mouth. "I have no *intention* of cooperating with a government down on Earth if it means harm coming to one of *my* employees."

Lan sensed the passion in Frau Köhler's tone.

It made her think of an overprotective mother.

The ones who they'd referred to as Tiger Mothers back in China.

Frau Köhler continued, "Obviously it will mean that you shall spend the rest of your life here—on the surface of the Moon." She seemed almost to revel in this silence, allowing it to draw out without any sign of it coming to an end. "However," she finally put in, "I *have* been informed of another proposal . . . another *plan*."

Lan's ears pricked up at this.

Her heart leaped to her throat.

"A 'plan' ?" she said, managing to raise her voice.

She wondered if she was still stunned by the—granted; *not-so-simple*—fact that Frau Köhler was literally speaking her language.

Again, Frau Köhler gave a warm smile.

A *reassuring* smile.

"I suppose that Patrick has said nothing of it to you—that he has mentioned nothing?"

"No."

"Gofreddo truly *has* found himself a friend for life in Mister Fourie."

"How so?"

Frau Köhler wiggled the tip of her nose as if she was relishing holding out the secret for just a few seconds more. Then she said, "What I am about to tell you is not to leave this room. I have been sworn to secrecy." Here she actually crossed her heart as if they were just a pair of teenage girls at some *sleepover*. "Gofreddo Zito is planning to explore the universe." She raised her eyes to Patrick, who was outside the office; out of earshot but still visible behind the glass. "And he wants *Patrick* to go along with him . . . he wants Patrick to be his *pilot*." She arched an eyebrow. "Because—goodness knows—from what I have heard of Gofreddo's antics with the Lunar Shuttles, he will *need* a good one."

A silence settled over the two of them.

Lan wondered if she was supposed to say something.

So she did.

"And, uh," Lan said, "where do *I* come in?"

Frau Köhler smiled more widely this time. "Well, he is looking for other crew, and, between you and me, I am sure that Gofreddo Zito could do with a little muscle. For when things 'get out of hand' on board, if you know what I mean?"

Lan felt herself sinking now.

Her heart beat faster.

She took in just what Frau Köhler was saying.

"One thing is obvious," Frau Köhler continued, "you will not be able to return to Earth—at least you will not be able to return to Earth without being incarcerated in some manner or other." She paused here for a long moment, then went on, "But perhaps I can aid you in *escaping* the Earth—escaping *capture* . . ."

Lan allowed Frau Köhler's words to sink in.

She *thought* she understood.

And yet it seemed so *far-fetched* . . . like what Frau Köhler said couldn't be true.

Her heart bobbed in her throat.

"I . . . this *offer*," Lan said. "What does it mean . . ." this time it was her turn to search for the words ". . . *practically* speaking?

Frau Köhler kept up her same easy smile. "Well—it means that you shall remain beneath the Celestial Stays Dome until the exploration mission is ready to take you away . . . to take you with them to go and see the universe."

Lan was rendered speechless.

An even longer silence settled on the office.

For a few moments, Lan was certain that her heart had just stopped completely.

Finally, from somewhere, Lan managed to find her voice.

"When . . . I do not . . ."

Frau Köhler waved her hand up in the air. "Think about it," she said, rising from the chair now. "You do not need to figure this all out at once. Give the offer time to settle." She came around the desk then stood before Lan. In a motherly manner, Frau Köhler reached out and settled her hand on Lan's shoulder. She gave her a squeeze. "This has been a difficult period for you, Lan, take your time. Think about it properly." Then she smiled. "Consider your options."

As she watched Frau Köhler stride out of the office, Lan analysed her parting words. It sounded almost as if there was a subtle threat there; as if there was an implied menace to what Frau Köhler said . . . in the eventuality of what would become of Lan if she failed to accept the offer.

Because what else was there for her now?

What choice *did* she have?

38

REPRIMAND

*L**an felt deeply self-conscious* as she climbed the Security HQ staircase. Her heart beat hard against her ribcage. She had turned over what she would do when she returned to work—when she returned to her day-to-day duties.

Frau Köhler had granted Lan a week's worth of leave following their meeting. Of course, she hadn't said so much to Lan personally—the last Lan had seen of Frau Köhler had been as she'd trod out of Mackenzie Angliss's office—but when Lan had returned to Security HQ the following day; to continue with her duty until told she was no longer required; the Link had informed her without delay that she had *no* duties to attend to.

This was Lan's first day back.

And she knew that it wouldn't be just a simple case of accepting her orders and carrying them out without question. It wouldn't be a simple case of her doing the 'professional' thing.

No, she was well aware of what had happened to her.

Of what she had done to others.

She sucked in a good lungful of air and then requested entrance to Supervisor Duval's office. It surprised her somewhat that he accepted her request without delay.

Before Lan really had time to process what'd just happened, she found herself standing before Duval. And, furthermore, that she was speechless.

Duval, she saw, right away, had his leg in a cast from where Lan had shot him with the blaster. He was working busily at the touch-screen at his desk; that same, familiar, vague look of confusion sketched all over his face—as if he was resolving the deepest, most oblique mysteries of the galaxy. While, in reality, he was most probably just trying to send Earthside Comms . . .

He took his time—about a minute by Lan's count—before he deigned to look up.

When he did so, his eyes were sunken in their sockets.

His skin seemed wrinkled rather than leathered today.

Everything about him seemed to have shrunk.

Lan had half expected him to make some show of fear toward her when she stood before him; wearing a look of desperation which dying animals under threat from some merciless predator might display. But, in actual fact, he just looked resilient.

Almost as if he was *willing* her to do him more damage.

He could take it.

Realising that the onus was on her to drive this interaction, Lan decided to speak.

"I'm . . . *sorry* about what happened."

Duval pursed his lips. "You mean you're sorry for *shooting* me?"

Catching a hint of humour in Duval's voice, Lan couldn't help but smile in reply. "Yeah," she said. "That was what I meant."

Duval flashed his eyebrows and then leaned back in his chair, discarding the touchscreen for a second. "Well, Niu, you heard what I said before—you know, all that *horseshit* about how I like people of action . . . I like people who aren't afraid to make decisions . . ." He tilted his head downward, to his leg in a cast and spoke to it, as if his leg was what he was addressing. "You come by here to apologise—to try and make things right?"

Here he looked up at her, and Lan noted that there was a touch of moisture in his eyes.

Not tears—*never tears* . . . not with Duval.

Lan sucked in a little more breath. "Something like that," she said.

Duval nodded to himself as if he was proving this right to some voice in his head he'd been arguing with. "Yeah, thought as much," he said, and then, his voice becoming gruffer—less introspective— added, "You should know better than to apologise to someone like me . . . to some old *fart* like me."

Lan suppressed the urge to smile until she realised that Duval himself was cracking a grin. It was kind of unnatural to see Duval smiling—at least, it wasn't something which Lan was accustomed to . . . she almost had the guts to tell him to stop . . .

Duval's smile dropped away slightly. He sighed out long and hard then met Lan's eye again. "No," he said, "I'm the one who should be apologising. Although—*granted*—I didn't know the full picture at the time. I didn't get the lowdown on your parents coming up here to kidnap you back to Earth."

"It wasn't their fault," Lan replied. "They were just going through with what they'd been strong-armed into doing. They had no choice." Here she felt her stomach sink slightly; her soaring, generally positive spirits becoming dampened. "When they return, they will end up just like me . . . they'll be kept under watch; never allowed their freedom." She waited a beat before uttering the word which seemed the only correct one. "They'll be treated like *traitors* until the day they die; never to be trusted."

Duval said nothing in response. He stared at his desktop, though not at the touchscreen. It seemed as if he was merely staring into mid-air; turning all these complicated 'worldly' matters over.

Finally, and not without a slight wince, Duval thrust himself up from his seat behind the desk. He grabbed hold of a cane leaning against the wall which Lan hadn't noticed when she'd come in. He staggered toward her, halting when he was three or four steps away.

"You know we're *fine*, kid," he said. "I don't wanna hear whatever it was that Frau Köhler spoke to you about, but if she says you're kosher then that's just fine by me."

He shifted his weight so that he leaned it onto the cane.

It took Lan a couple of seconds to realise that he was stretching his hand out to her.

She took it off him.

Gave it a shake.

When he released her from his firm grip, Lan realised that she herself was smiling. And that she felt *warm* inside. As if nothing could ever touch her again.

Whatever the real danger—whatever the *complications*—she was certain that it was over now. And, what was more, she could be certain that she had chosen the right path.

To think that she might've followed her parents into the ROCAF—that she might've given her life to her country . . . just what would it have meant to her life?

Would she have been chewed up and spat out so indignantly like her parents apparently had?

Made use of and then thrown away?

Those were thoughts for another time.

Now she just needed to enjoy her life.

In many ways, it seemed as if it was just beginning.

As Duval turned his back on her, returning to his desk, he spoke over his shoulder. "Take the day off, Niu." He flapped his hand at her. "Go to the gym—*take a swim*—whatever it is you do with that downtime of yours."

Lan parted her lips to protest.

She had already spent a whole week off duty and it seemed like an undeserved extravagance.

But, before she could point this out, Duval spoke in his gravelly, no-nonsense tone.

"*Dismissed!*"

The volume of his voice took Lan so off guard that she immediately retreated from the office; no thoughts of further insubordination on her mind.

39

DECISION TIME

*L*an *had hardly got back* to her room in the Basements when the Link informed her that she had a visitor. She thought hard about whether or not she was supposed to be having 'visitors' . . . it seemed almost as if she didn't *deserve* a visitor.

Perhaps it was just how she had conditioned herself during this peculiar week off.

She wasn't certain who she'd expected at her door, although, if pressed, she never would've thought it to be Alicia and Louise.

Lan had done her best to keep her head down throughout the week; not wanting to cause any waves; to drag up any drama besides that which she'd already caused. She had somehow assumed she had ended up in poor standing with these two women, but now, it seemed—at least from the ripe grins spreading their cheeks—they had never had so much as a disagreement in all their lives.

Straight away, Lan noticed the wicker picnic basket hanging down at Louise's side, of course.

And she couldn't help but breathe in the smell of what she was sure to be Moon Cakes . . . those delicious treats which her family —not her parents, but her *aunts and uncles*—would prepare for Chinese New Year.

"We thought we owed you an apology," Alicia said, offering the basket to Lan.

Lan took it from her. "Uh . . . *thanks*," she replied, taking the basket, and not knowing quite what to do with it once she had it.

"We talked about it," Louise said, picking up where Alicia had left off, "and we decided that it was important that we remained in good standing with someone we're likely to spend the rest of our lives with."

Lan felt as if she'd been punched in the stomach. "What? What do you mean?"

"We mean," Alicia put in, this time taking it upon herself to speak, "that since we're all going to be travelling on the same ship together—blasting into Outer Space—we should all do our best to be friends." She gave a wide smile at the end of this statement, and then held her finger to her lips. "You have to promise to keep it a secret, though . . . Gofreddo would get *awfully* upset if he found news leaking out to someone not involved in the mission."

Lan felt confused, and then she turned to Louise. "And . . . what about *you*—are you coming on the mission too?"

Louise nodded. "Me and Njhay—we got the invite a few weeks back." She shrugged. "Why Gofreddo thinks that *I'll* be any use beats me . . . maybe he just asked me along because he wanted a botanist in Njhay."

Alicia gave Louise a sidelong shoulder barge. "Shut up," she said. "I already told you that he has you lined up to be his First Mate . . . or even Captain, depending on how Gofreddo's planning on eventually organising things."

"That's easy to say for the Ship's *Cook*," Louise shot back. "I mean, if we don't do what *you* say then we go hungry . . . or, worse, if we really piss you off then you'll slip poison into our oatmeal, or something . . ."

Lan couldn't help but grin at the back-and-forth between Alicia and Louise. She noted how they had dropped that happy-go-lucky front which they always seemed to present to strangers—to those on the *outside*. Lan couldn't help wondering if—maybe—she hadn't finally found where she belonged. Where she *really* belonged.

On a whim, she said, "I guess I'll have the freedom to break anyone's arm who needs it breaking, right?"

For a second, both Alicia and Louise stared at her with stern seriousness.

And then they both cracked up.

All three of them stood about, laughing and joking over what would occur in their near-future . . . just how near, Lan didn't have the nerve to ask.

As everyone on Earth knew, it wasn't a question of investing in the technology of such a mission—of building a spaceship from scratch—it was more a case of *funding* . . . and Gofreddo—or, more exactly, his father, Costantino—had that . . . and *in spades* . . .

Once Louise and Alicia had said what they needed to say, they left her in peace. And, indeed, when Lan opened up the picnic basket, she found dozens of beautifully crafted Moon Cakes.

She lost herself in nostalgia, and memory—and not a few tears —as she ate her way through a couple of them.

When the Link advised her that there was someone else at her door, she had the urge to request that they go away; that they leave her in peace.

All that changed, however, when the Link informed her who it was.

Patrick.

Her heart fluttering up to her throat, and with a quick glance at herself in the mirror—to make sure that she didn't have any pieces of Moon Cake sticking around her mouth—she jigged over to the door and opened up.

Sure enough, Patrick Fourie stood there.

He smiled wide at her.

She took in his strawberry-blond hair.

And his muscular stature.

He was still dressed in his grey-white flight overalls.

"You'll never guess what," he said, taking a step into the room.

On impulse, Lan took a step back . . . allowing him in. "What?" she asked.

He gave her a sly grin, and then, much to her surprise, said—in *perfect* Shanghainese—"I got given the day off too." On seeing her reaction, he smiled wider still, then said, this time in English, "I got the details of Frau Köhler's teacher." He jerked his thumb over his shoulder, apparently indicating his own quarters in the Basements. "She set me up with some introductory materials." He cocked his head to one side, and then said—again in Shanghainese—"What do you think?"

Unable to hold herself back any longer, Lan threw her arms about his neck, sifting her hands through his thick hair . . . tugging his face down to hers.

She kissed him hard on the mouth.

Absorbed his warmth.

When they separated, their eyes still fixed upon one another, Patrick smiled more widely still, then said, "Guess we're all set for a little journey, huh?"

Feeling her heart tapping faster all the time, Lan couldn't help but sense the raw positivity flowing through her veins. Since she would've found it very difficult to disagree with Patrick, she just pushed herself upward once again.

And kissed him harder still.

Her life—it seemed—had worked out in the end.

THE END

AUTHOR'S NOTE

Thank you for taking the time to read one of my books. If you would like to hear about my latest releases you can sign up for my newsletter here: www.essiepowers.com

Thanks for reading!

Essie Powers

Moon Struck
The Third Lunar Lovescape Novel

Copyright © Essie Powers, 2016.
Published by DIB Books
All rights reserved.